To Antonio Rendon

Enjoy

Dark Matter Universe Series
Alex Twice Abducted

TL Walker

Copyright © 2015 T. L. Walker

All rights reserved. Except as permitted under the U.S. Copyright Act of 1976, no part of this publication may be reproduced, distributed or transmitted in any form or by any means, or stored in a database or retrieval system without the prior written permission of the author or publisher.

This is a work of fiction. Names, characters, places and incidents are products of the author's imagination or are used fictitiously and are not to be construed as real. Any resemblance to actual events, locales, organizations, or persons, living or deceased, is entirely coincidental.

ISBN-13: **9781947133013**

Photo Credits for title page:
Sword in title - "Albion_Thegn_Viking_Sword_1" "Søren Niedziell"
"https://www.flickr.com/photos/albioneurope/" Cropped and edited
Back cover
Zeghes - "Bottlenose Dolphin (Tursiops Truncatus), Marineland, Antibes" "Spencer Wright"
"https://www.flickr.com/photos/spencer77/" Cropped and edited
All under license "https://creativecommons.org/licenses/by/2.0/legalcode"

DEDICATION

This book's dedicated to my fans and many more: Porsche Appleman, my first fan and a wonderful fan, may all my future fans be just as fanatical; to my two daughters, Lynn and Laura, who first suggested I write stories for others to read and enjoy; and to my wonderful wife, Debbie, her forbearance for years with my writing struggles allowed for the opportunity to continue to fruition. All of your support and belief in me and in this project has been instrumental in its success.

This book wouldn't exist without the hard work and sincere efforts of Porsche Appleman, Laurie Rosin, Irene Roth Luvaul, Judy Walker, and Debbie Walker. The hundreds of hours you spent laboring with me were appreciated more than you'll ever know.

A very special thanks to a local author, Connie Jasperson, who has been there for me as a volunteer editor, fan, friend, and mentor.

I want to thank the many who helped me with the research. The Kalasha researcher, Wynne Maggi, for her invaluable help in understanding the Kalasha people. Lee Merrick of Alaska Falcons helped me to get the characterization of Ytell and the other alien raptors right. When I write about the alien raptors I think of his beautiful Gyrfalcons.

Then there are the countless many who patiently listened to me talk about it and read portions to give me feedback. You know who you are and I hope you find those who'll help you with your dreams.

Last, but not least is a great thanks to Laura for helping me finish this project.

Pronunciations

- A'idah – Ī ē duh

  Twelve year old girl from Northwest Pakistan, one of Alex's best friends and a member of his flock

- Amable – Ă muh bull

  The leader of the aliens abducting and training the Earthlings

- Coruscated – kor uh skāt ed

  Definition: *flashed or sparkled*

- Ekbal – ĕhk bal

  Twelve year old boy from southern India, a member of Alex's flock

- Gaahr – Gahr; simply ah with a hard g sound in front followed by a long r sound, like in *arrrgh!*

  A species of Deem

- Gagugugul – Gah goo goo gull

  A Gaahr

- Gursha – Ger shuh

  The nurse of Alex's flock

- Haal – Hăl

  A Dwarf (What a strange universe)

- Heyeze – Hī ēz

  An evil philosopher of the dolphins

- Hheilea – Hī lē uh

  A Kimley fifteen year old girl

- Hhy Soaley – Hī sōl ē

  Hheilea, disguised as a boy

- Hymeron – Hī mer uhn

  Hheilea's brother

- Lepercaul – lĕp r call

  An alien species

- Lillyputi – lĭl ē poo tē

  A wonderful desert, dangerously addictive for humans

- Maleky – Muh lĕk ē

  The most evil person in the galaxy

- Numbel – Nuhm bell

  A Dwarf

- Osamu – ō săm oo: the oo is the same sound in boo

  A Japanese man and a member of Alex's flock

- Sabu – Să boo

    A snow leopard and a member of Alex's flock

- Skyler – skī ler

    A Blue Hyacinth Macaw and a member of Alex's flock

- Tierce – tirs; pronounced like tear plus a c sound like in pierce

    A fencing term referring to a type of block

- Twarbie – twăr bē

    A Winkle female, who looks like she might be close to Alex's age

- Vapuc – vă pook

    The result of dark matter affecting a living creature to allow it to alter the laws of the universe

- Ytell – yuh těl

    He looks like Earth's raptors and is the leader of Alex's flock and the leader of the other raptors

- Zeghes – zā s

    A six month old dolphin who is a member of Alex's flock

What follows is the best thanks I can give. Please read on. Laugh, cry, and think. Be amazed and fascinated. Enjoy.

CONTENTS

1	Alien Abduction	Pg 1
2	Zeghes The dolphin	Pg 3
3	Zeghes And A'idah Get To Know Alex	Pg 8
4	Zeghes Saves Alex	Pg 15
5	What Will Be Done With Alex?	Pg 23
6	Hheilea	Pg 37
7	Practice	Pg 52
8	Sword Fighting	Pg 63
9	The First Fight	Pg 71
0	T'wasn't-to-be-is	Pg 81
11	Control	Pg 89
	Excerpt from the Novel 'Alex Inner Voice.'	

Chapter One
Alien Abduction

Unconscious, Alex lay alone in the wet grass. Fog swirled around him. For a year, he'd been fighting the inevitable. The doctors had said he was dying of unknown causes, but today for the first time his illness took a back seat. The lack of control over his life wasn't new, but the strangeness was.

The sound of sirens drew Alex back to consciousness. He opened his eyes to fog. Frantic, he tried to get up, but he couldn't move his body. A scream burst from him. "Aaaaah! Help!" The sirens came closer.

A man called out, "Who's out there?!"

"Over here! Help me!" He still couldn't move.

"Keep calling," the man cried. "This strange fog is making it hard to find you!"

"I can't move! Please...please help me!"

"That's it," The man said. "I'm getting closer. Keep talking. Everything's going to be okay."

Alex knew he wouldn't be saved. How he knew, he couldn't tell, but he just knew that the man wasn't going to get to him in time. Yet, fear pushed another scream out of him. "Hurry!"

The man spoke in calm, comforting tones. "It's okay. I see you. Everything's going to be fine."

No, it wasn't. Again, Alex screamed, "It's too late!"

"Calm down! Look at me!" The man reached for him.

The ground fell away from under Alex. The man's face registered shock, and he jumped for him. For a second - just a second - the man had a hold of his shoe.

For a brief moment hope stirred in Alex, but cold winds of reality stopped it.

"I've got you. I won't let go," the man said.

Alex stopped rising. The man pulled on him and brought his other hand around to grab at Alex's thin leg, and Alex saw a strange look appear on the man' face. It looked like fear. It also looked like determination. He couldn't pinpoint which of the two it was. For a long second they stared at each other.

A scream suddenly erupted from the man. "No!" he cried out as Alex's shoe ripped from his grasp.

Cold, wind, and misty tendrils of fog streamed past as sunshine struck his face. Blinded by the light, and in a state of fear and confusion one paralyzing thought suddenly came to mind - he was being abducted! Suddenly, something above him drew near, blocking the sun. In a flash of an instant Alex was pulled towards the object, then- POP - he was sucked into an entrance tube! Lights flashed quickly as he continued his journey upwards.

He popped from the tube, and a cacophony of sounds assaulted him as his body settled onto a large, yellow disc. A sharp pungent smell, like ozone, assailed his nose, and he sneezed. After rolling over, Alex struggled to his knees. A shimmering wall of yellow light rose from the edge of his disc. Placing his hand on the wall of light he felt it give a little before hardening.

Fighting back his terror, Alex looked around. Other discs of different colors with their own walls, prisons of light, floated around him. Each prison held a person or animal.

Above the disc nearest to Alex, a dolphin floated in the air before him. They stared at each other, curiously. How did you get abducted, and what do you think of all this and being given the ability to move in the air, like it's water?

Chapter Two
Zeghes the Dolphin

Zeghes had been swimming in the warm sea water. Two-leggeds had been with his pod. They'd come in their noisy wave maker. He'd gotten to surf on the wake it created and had checked out the clumsy two leggeds when they jumped into the water. They were funny, clumsy swimmers.

How Zeghes wished he could learn more about them and maybe even ride in the wave maker. Too bad the two-leggeds didn't know how to talk dolphin.

After the visitors left, Zeghes looked for his older cousin. He remembered in disgust how he'd left to live in the males' pod. *Hmph.* The memory angered Zeghes. He was old enough to leave the babies and females, too. He didn't need his mom anymore.

He was Zeghes and could take care of himself. Slowly, he edged away from his mother and the rest of the pod.

He wasn't afraid of sharks. The young dolphin had watched when the adults teamed up to kill a shark. They'd rammed it until the shark stopped swimming and slowly sank to the bottom, trailing blood from its gills. If any shark bothered him, he'd ram it too. Zeghes didn't want to remember the other part of what had happened.

His mother kept telling him he wasn't ready for the dangers. He'd show her. He didn't need her or this pod.

Faintly, Zeghes felt something.... He wasn't sure what had caught his interest. He turned his head back and forth. He didn't use his sonar but just listened. He had it - the sound of splashing in the distance! His mother, aunts, cousins and others in his local pod were busy and hadn't noticed Zeghes edging away.

Something else nipped at his attention. He wasn't sure what. An unusual feeling, maybe trouble...? Zeghes couldn't see any sharks with his sonar. Everything would be fine.

With a burst of speed, the young dolphin glided easily through the water. Zeghes leapt above the surface, whistled, and twisted in the air with great exuberation. Whatever was out there better lookout - Zeghes was on patrol! He could control and protect his own life without the pod and his mother. Just before he landed, the dolphin spotted movement on the water's surface far ahead of him. Something swung up into the air and splashed.

Splashing back into the water himself, Zeghes fired off more sonar pulses. This time, he was rewarded with a faint image. In excitement, he recognized the form of a two legged swimming on the water's surface. Something else off to his left only slightly registered. Again, the odd, unfamiliar feeling of something going to happen flashed through his head. He'd never had that kind of feeling about the future before and for just a second he considered it. Zeghes charged forward, whistling out his name and listening for a response, but none came from the clumsy two-legged creature.

In a flash, Zeghes was close to the swimmer. He carefully studied it, using his sonar to look through its strange coverings. It was a female. The clumsy swimmer stopped and held her head up out of the water.

Zeghes porpoised his head up out of the water, too. He turned his head from the side to better look at her. For a long moment they looked at each other. The young dolphin chattered away hoping for an intelligent response, but the female just made unintelligible noises.

Suddenly, the two legged's eyes grew wide.

How did it do that?

The female jerked a forelimb up out of the water pointing out past Zeghes, and it let out what really seemed like some kind of distress call. Then it flipped over and swam away.

Curious, Zeghes fired off sonar to check out his surroundings. Panicked, he surged forward. The image of a huge shark forging straight for him flashed into his mind.

Terror gripped the young dolphin. The memory of the other shark killing a baby dolphin flooded him with fear. The adults hadn't been able save it. The horrible memory persisted.

He heard the answering clicks and whistles of his pod. Zehges

Chapter two

hadn't even realized he'd sent out a distress call. Even in his panic, he continued watching the shark and the rest of his surroundings, preparing to take evasive action at any moment. Relief began to wash over him, and the terror ebbed. The shark hadn't changed course to follow him.

Another realization hit. The terror came back. Again, the young dolphin could see the memory of how the shark had savagely tore into the side of the young dolphin. It had shaken the baby until finally the shark ripped a huge chunk out of its side. The baby dolphin had twisted, shook, blood stained the water, and it went limp.

This female would die. It was clumsy and swam way too slowly. These thoughts and more raced through Zeghes mind. Fear won the race, but raw determination shoved itself forward.

No! He wouldn't let this shark kill another! Somehow, he'd stop it. Zeghes hadn't even thought about making a tight turn back onto a collision course. He knew he had to stop the shark's attack or the female two legged would die. Somehow, he had to hit the shark hard enough to injure it or knock it off course. Zeghes couldn't let her die.

The small dolphin dug deep for more strength. He had to hit the shark with enough force - he simply had to! With all his strength, he raced through the water. Somewhere in his mind, in response to his need, a new ability emerged. It came from the same part of his mind that had already changed once, giving him imperfect warnings about the future. These changes to his mind were caused by something he knew nothing about.

Zeghes raced on his interception course coming from below to hit the underbelly of the shark. He had wanted to hit it in the gills, but there was no time. The swimmer was just feet away. The dolphin's world narrowed to the demanding need to hit the shark hard and to shove it away from the female.

Something invisible shoved through the water just in front of Zeghes, pulling him after it. The force hit the shark, blasting it up and out into the air. It tumbled. Zeghes, too, shot up into the air. Both of them came back down with the young dolphin painfully slamming onto the much bigger shark.

Pain threatened the dolphin's ability to swim. Though dazed, he managed to get back to the surface where he could breathe.

Fortunately, the shark was only barely able to swim. Blood leaked from its gills as it disappeared into the depths.

Trying to rest while dealing with debilitating pain, Zeghes couldn't help but stir at the sound of his pod calling out his name. They knew what had happened. He was a hero. He'd saved the female.

Another odd sensation whispered in his mind.

Warnings from his pod whistled and clicked at him. The last thing he heard from his mother - "Zeghes!"

He suddenly felt the waters divide away from him. All Zeghes could do was drop his lower jaw in shock. As the water continued to divide cold air ripped by him. To calm himself he began to whistle. First he whistled his mother's name, then other important members of his pod.

Terrible distress tore at him, but the newly recognized hero struggled not to give in to fear. An amazing view gave food to both. The sea below and the beach with its dunes.... For the first time he saw strange things beyond them. But all too soon that disappeared. Sights, sounds, and other sensations even more confusing overwhelmed him. He lay on a hard, unyielding surface. Creatures he'd never seen before worked around him. He felt something slipping over and molding to his skin. The creatures moved away, leaving him with a feeling of strange, unnatural calmness. It didn't feel normal. A coloured wall - slightly transparent - rose up all around him.

A shudder went through Zeghes' body at the terrible sight of a seven foot tall bird with a dangerous beak looking at him. It had the look of a dangerous predator, maybe another type of shark.

His body suddenly rose up off the hard surface. The biggest shock and surprise came from his body moving in the air as if he was in the water. Carefully, he used this new ability to explore his cage. Outside it, the strange creatures continued to work. Other strange creatures were placed in similar prisons to his own. There were two-legged creatures being placed into prisons also.

One last prisoner, a two-legged, was placed into a yellow prison.

The new two-legged looked at him, and Zeghes looked intently back. He was a male and ill. The dolphin needed to get to him. Sick shouldn't be by themselves. Zeghes rammed the wall of light again and again, trying to get out. One of these big birds might decide to eat the boy. Sharks eat the sick. He had to protect him.

As Zeghes fought, the boy left his disc with a white-haired creature's help. From above came loud, piercing calls. The dolphin didn't think they were happy about the boy getting out of his prison. One of the giant birds, a raptor, launched from a perch to dive toward the boy. The bird's going to attack. Zeghes had to get free. The young dolphin battered himself harder against the wall of light, ignoring the pain until darkness swallowed up his awareness.

Chapter Three
Zeghes and A'idah get to know Alex

Zeghes, the dolphin, swam through the air. He didn't need the small, bouncing ball of light guiding them through the spaceship, because he'd created a map in his head of this part of the labyrinth of halls. From behind him came the echoing sounds of A'idah's footsteps. The changes in the last five days overwhelmed him. He could understand what everyone said, including the aliens. Zeghes didn't know if he could trust them, even though the aliens kept saying, "We are trying to help you." They were helping the boy, Alex. Zeghes also loved the transparent suit the aliens gave him. From behind him, A'idah said, "Wait up. I have to see him first."

Zeghes twisted back in the air to face her. "Stop trying to tell me what to do. Girls aren't supposed to order guys about."

A'idah ducked past him to enter the nurses' clinic. "Get used to it, Zeghes. I'm not a dolphin."

Gursha, the four-armed nurse greeted them, "You're just in time." She turned to Alex. "Alex, wake-up. Some of your flock members are here to meet you."

Alex lay surrounded by a blue haze, except for the pink haze around his head. He floated in the haze about three feet off the ground. Alex blinked and turned his head toward them.

"Hi there, Alex," Zeghes said. "Don't worry about any danger. Zeghes is here. That's me. The girl is A'idah. You go ahead and talk to her. I'm going to patrol the area for sharks."

"Uh, hi," Alex said weakly. "There was another dream before this." He paused and then said, "I slugged a giant bird."

"Hi," A'idah said and turned to Gursha. "Are you sure he's ready for company?"

"He's just a bit groggy. He needs to get up for a while."

Zeghes had paused for a moment, as he listened to the

conversation, before he swam away to patrol.

"I like this dream. It's better than the ..." Alex's words faded as Zeghes moved farther from the clinic. Moving his head back and forth, he built a map in his head of the passageways as he swam. The spaceship's rooms and passageways seemed kinda like a coral reef without water. A semi-translucent creature, eight-feet tall and four-feet wide, waddled around a corner of the passageway. "You need to scoot over to make room for me to get by," Zeghes said.

The creature lifted a thick arm and pointed at Zeghes. "You're one of the new Earthlings. I don't scoot over."

Then the creature waved a hand, and Zeghes found himself pushed against the ceiling, as the creature started to thump past below him. Zeghes remembered using a similar type of force back on Earth to shove a shark out of the water, before the aliens abducted him. He shoved back at the creature, pushing him down onto the floor. Immediately, Zeghes swam toward the clinic. He didn't think all of these aliens on the space ship were very nice. It was just like in the ocean - some dolphins were bullies too. He remembered hearing stories about dolphins across the ocean, killing porpoises just for the fun of it. As he approached the clinic A'idah's voice roused him from his own thoughts.

"You froze water and made yourself lighter?" She asked.

"I guess so."

Zeghes swam back into the room. That must've been Alex. "All safe. No sharks," he declared.

Alex stood beside A'idah, wearing cream-colored loose pants and shirt like the other humans. "A dolphin - right here in the air!" he marvelled. "He's swimming in the air and talking to me!"

"He's been given some kind of fancy suit," A'idah said as she smiled at Alex. "It makes him able to swim through the air just like he's still in the water."

"What makes him able to talk?" Alex asked.

A'idah pointed toward her ear. "I guess you haven't heard about squirts yet."

"What're squirts?"

"Small organisms placed behind our ears. They make it so we can understand the animals and the aliens," A'idah said.

Alex's hand started to move up to his ear. "This is crazy. Are there really sharks up here?"

"On Earth, we always watch for sharks," Zeghes said. "I'm told there are no sharks here. But I still watch." He especially watched the raptors, as they seemed like sharks.

"Can I touch you?" Alex asked Zeghes.

"Sure thing."

"I can feel the suit you're wearing, and yet it lets my hand through to touch your skin. This is amazing. Gursha says I'm going to live and ..." Tears began to cascade down his face. Zeghes rubbed against him in an effort to console him.

A'idah put her arms around Zeghes and Alex. "Hey, I understand," she admitted. "I bawled like a baby after I began to move and feel again."

"Thanks for holding me," Alex sniffed while straightening and gathering himself. "Sorry I lost it."

Zeghes had watched two white-haired creatures, similar to the humans, sneak into the clinic. Now, they ran out of the room.

A'idah looked down at her feet and then at Alex's feet. "Wait!"

She spoke too late. Alex started to take a step. "When did those —?" He tipped forward, thin arms windmilling, and grabbed for A'idah. Missing, he fell down. "Ah!"

Laughing, A'idah said, "Sorry for laughing about your shoes being tied together. The Soaley boys seem to victimize everyone. They're Kimleys, one of the many different kinds of aliens you're going to meet."

Zeghes backed up, looking after the Kimleys. He'd seen one of those creatures the first day, but A'idah called them both boys. It was probably just another thing he was confused about.

The sound of heavy footsteps came from the doorway. Zeghes turned to see Ytell, a dark blue, almost black, raptor entering the clinic. A'idah stepped between Alex and Ytell, craned her neck to look up at Ytell's face, and said, "You came too soon."

"Look out, A'idah," Alex said, scrambling to his feet. "It's the alien that bit me."

Ytell, with one of his yellow and red eyes, tipped his head to consider A'idah. "I'm sorry. Haven't you explained to Alex what's going on?"

It was the shark. Zeghes dove at Ytell, but too late, he saw Ytell's hooked beak slash down at him. Again the young dolphin remembered the shark savaging the baby dolphin, but the beak

Chapter 3

stopped just before cutting into him. Zeghes rammed into Ytell. "You need to leave Alex alone. He's still sick. You can't catch us and shove us around like you do. It isn't right."

Ytell backed up, and Zeghes hung in the air. Feelings of confusion stirred within Zeghes as he realized Ytell had chosen not to defend himself. He moved his head back and forth, examining Ytell with his sonar. He could see broken ribs. Why was the shark standing still? Meanwhile, Alex and A'idah spoke at the same time.

A'idah poked at Ytell's dark-red breast with her finger. "Zeghes is right. You need to leave Alex alone. We're informing him about what's going on."

Alex hopped forward. "Don't hurt my friend," he said, falling against A'idah, taking both of them down onto Ytell's scaly, blue feet.

Gursha bustled forward, and Zeghes drifted out of her way. Her voice resonated with authority and irritation. "You Earthlings be quiet and wait. Ytell, you're hurt. Come over here."

Shaking his head, Ytell pulled his feet out from under the two humans. "I can—"

Gursha interrupted him with a glare and pointed to a pattern on the floor. After taking a step, Ytell paused and shuffled the rest of the way to the pattern.

A blue haze rose up lifting Ytell. It turned pink around the area Zeghes had hit. Gursha muttered to herself, one set of hands on her hips and with the other set reached into the haze. "You didn't have to let him break your ribs."

"Zeghes could've gotten hurt, and fighting with him would slow down his acclimatization," Ytell stated. "We've already caused him trouble adjusting. He thinks I'm the equivalent of a shark. For Earth's sake, all of the Earthlings must progress quickly."

Gursha pulled her hands out of the haze as some of the pink turned to blue. "Okay, your ribs have begun to knit. I don't suppose you'll stay until they're completely mended?"

"No." The blue haze faded away, lowering Ytell to the ground. He stretched and slightly opened his wings. Shaking his feathers, he closed his wings back against his body. "Your healing me was a great idea. That injury would've affected my ability to train the Earthlings."

Gursha frowned and stepped closer to him. "Everything isn't

about training the Earthlings. Don't fly during the next few days and come back if it starts hurting again."

"Thank you," Ytell said.

Gursha said, "Of course you won't come back because of a little pain, you stubborn bird. And since you're too stubborn to stay until you're healed, you need to leave. This has been too much excitement for my other patient."

Ytell turned to Alex. "I'm Ytell, your flock leader. I'll see you tomorrow morning." He left with a swish of his feathers.

Watching in confusion, Zeghes had a new thought form about Ytell. Maybe Ytell is like the dominant dolphins and not a shark, except for the fact that the big male dolphins wouldn't have let Zeghes get away with ramming one of them. Even the females wouldn't have let him. Zeghes looked at the two humans. A'idah and Alex were still on the floor, watching as Ytell left.

A'idah laughed a short nervous laugh and said, "We showed him."

A grin replaced the scowl on Alex's face, as he joined A'idah in laughter. "I guess we did."

Gursha came over and helped A'idah and Alex up off the floor.

"Thanks, Gursha." Alex said, as he stood to his feet.

The nurse continued to hold A'idah by the arm, and spoke to Alex. "Do you see that pattern on the floor?"

"Yes."

"Go sit down in the air over it. The holo-field will respond to your thoughts and support you."

"Okay." Alex turned around and awkwardly sat in midair. A blue haze appeared around his body, supporting him in a sitting position. "What did Ytell mean about causing Zeghes trouble?"

A'idah tried to pull away from Gursha. "After Zeghes was torn from his pod in the abduction he saw you fight Ytell, one of the abductors. That caused him to bond with you and me as his new pod. It means we're his new family. However, it also caused his aggression towards Ytell. For now, he's thinking Ytell is another type of shark. The PETA rep says Ytell has to allow it, per a signed agreement. She says Zeghes will eventually heal from the abduction trauma, and the aggression toward Ytell will stop."

Zeghes started to speak, but changed his mind as he tried to sort out what he'd just heard.

"So now you, Zeghes, and I are family? Alex asked. I like that idea. I'll try and be a good big brother, for him and you."

Gursha shook A'idah by the arm she held. "A'idah?"

"What?" A'idah tried again to pull away.

"Young lady," Gursha said, glowering at A'idah. "You forget your responsibility to Alex. We talked about this during your visits here."

Alex looked back and forth between the two of them. A'idah opened her mouth to reply, but Gursha held up a hand, keeping two firmly on her hips. "Don't excuse yourself to me. Tell Alex what he needs to know."

A'idah looked at Alex and down at his feet. "I'm sorry, I should've talked about this before Ytell arrived. I told him I would."

"What?" Alex asked.

"Get on with it," Gursha said.

A'idah looked up into Alex's eyes. "I knew Ytell was just coming to talk to you. He has checked up on you every day. He's been concerned about your health. Also, he wasn't attacking you on the day of your abduction, and he won't attack you now. They needed to finish sorting out the flocks, and Alex, you were holding things up. They couldn't leave Earth until they finished. Ytell is worried about having enough time to help us. They are in a hurry to get us to our new academy. We must accomplish something before the year is up, or the aliens will give up on Earth. This would mean everyone on Earth dies."

A'idah paused, breathing deeply. Her eyes glistened. Gursha pulled her close. "If you had said that sooner, Alex wouldn't have reacted to Ytell the way he did, which might've kept Zeghes from attacking Ytell."

"I'm sorry … for not telling him sooner," A'idah said.

"That's enough visiting for now. I want all of you out," Gursha said.

"I should stay with Alex," Zeghes said. "Sick pod members should not be left alone."

"He'll be fine, Zeghes," Gursha said.

A'idah paused at the door. "Thanks for standing up to Ytell for me, Alex."

Alex said, "Family has to stand up for each other, and don't worry about not having told me all that stuff before Ytell arrived.

When I saw him again, I still would've reacted the same way."

Again, Zeghes wanted to speak up. He'd rammed Ytell. Why didn't A'idah thank him? Outside in the hall, he realized A'idah wasn't with him. Twisting around, he saw her standing still by the door of the clinic. Gliding back, he bumped A'idah. "What are you doing?"

A'idah looked at Zeghes for a moment before saying, "I don't want to leave, but I guess we'll see him tomorrow."

Chapter Four
Zeghes Saves Alex

The next day, Zeghes hurried ahead of the flock. Ahead of him the small bouncing ball of light sped up to keep pace with him. Today, the flock had their first training session. Zeghes had been staying near Alex and A'idah, but his sonar told him a huge space was at the end of the hall, and he couldn't wait to explore it. Speeding faster, he rocketed through a doorway and into the Hall of Flight. A vast open space greeted him. He hadn't realized how suffocating the tight confines of rooms and passageways had been. Joy filled him, and he did barrel rolls out into the middle of the huge room. In the distance, he could see other Raptors and their flocks. In his joy, he didn't hear a voice calling to him.

"Zeghes! I said get back here!" Ytell yelled the second time.

The young dolphin looked back to the entrance. The rest of his flock had gathered on the balcony there, and he went over their names in his head. Sabu, a snow leopard, chased after Skyler, a blue hyacinth macaw, as the bird flew just out of her paw's reach. Ekbal, an inquisitive, dark-skinned boy, was squatted on the ground examining something. Alex and A'idah stood together by the doorway. Peter, the flock's skeptic, stood with arms crossed, scowling. The last member stood close to Ytell. He was an older human man called Osamu, and the way he looked at Zeghes chased away all of his good feelings. Osamu ordered all the nonhuman Earthlings around, but worse than this he had eaten dolphin meat in the past. Zeghes slapped at the air with his tail in annoyance, then swam back toward the flock. As he swam closer, he heard Ytell start another boring lecture. "The green areas with yellow circles are bubble platforms. Everyone, find a circle to stand on. That goes for you, too, Zeghes. Just float over one."

Ytell nodded in approval at the flock members. "Stay still until the bubble forms. These are special bubbles used to determine the individual's ability to react to Dark Matter. The more you react to Dark Matter, the better you will be able to control the movement of your bubble with your thoughts. Not everyone can use these bubbles, but anyone can use normal bubbles."

"What's the red circle?" Ekbal asked.

"It's broken," Ytell answered.

Zeghes saw bubbles growing up from the circles to surround each flock member. What was that odd tingling sensation? Looking down, he saw a bubble rapidly encase him.

The bubbles had an iridescent sheen, just like soap bubbles. Zeghes soared into the middle of the hall in his. Others floated up and moved slowly away. Shouting interrupted the scene and drew his attention.

Peter pushed at the wall of his bubble. "Protect me from this evil, Lord! Keep these demons from me! With thy power, these demons have no control over me!"

Over the yelling came Ytell's firm voice, "You have been identified as someone, who through a natural force, not a spiritual force, does many things mostly unexplained by our science. I don't have time to waste. This will prove if Dark Matter affects you."

With that, Ytell partially opened his wings, which then spanned twenty feet. A mighty beat of his wings caused a gust of air to push Peter's bubble over the edge of the platform, causing it to fall. Everyone heard a short scream. A moment later, Peter rocketed back up in his bubble.

"What have you done to me?" Peter sobbed. "I thought you were interested in what I told you about God, but then you did this."

"I was intrigued about what you said, but you need to listen me," Ytell said.

The rest of the flock bobbled, soared, or gently moved through the air in their bubbles, except for Alex.

"It's easy. Just make your bubble move," Osamu said. "It responds to your thoughts."

"Come on, Alex. It's fun," A'idah said.

Zeghes moved closer to Alex. Something wasn't right. Alex jumped up and down, and his bubble moved a little. He charged forward in his bubble and off the edge. His bubble fell toward the

Chapter 4

distant floor.

"Ahhh!" Alex screamed.

In his bubble Zeghes dashed below Alex and bounced into his bubble, causing it to rise. He continued bumping into Alex's bubble until it finally bounced back onto the platform and dissipated, leaving him sprawled on the ground at Ytell's feet.

Zeghes spun in his bubble. That was fun. He liked saving Alex.

Turning to Alex, Ytell commanded, "Go stand out of the way by the entrance." He then looked at Zeghes. "Thanks. If necessary, I would've caught Alex, but you used great initiative."

"No! I'm trying again," Alex said.

"Alex." Ytell leaned his head down toward him. "Fighting with me is a waste of our time."

"I'll teach you to spin me." Skyler's voice came from the middle of the hall, snatching Zeghes' attention. He turned to see Sabu had just spun Skyler's bubble with a swat from a magically enlarged paw. It made Zeghes think of the rough games he played with the other young dolphins. As everyone watched, Skyler let Sabu close in behind him. It became evident he could move faster as he rolled up and over, coming down right behind Sabu.

With a see-how-you-like-this motion, Skyler clamped onto Sabu's bubble with what looked like an incredibly large bill and shook it.

"Everyone look at those two," Ytell stated. "They're using an innate ability to do two forms of *vapuc*, illusion and force. Vapuc is not magic or a spiritual force of any kind. Vapuc is what we call the things you can do if you react to Dark Matter. When we get to the academy, you'll learn how force works. How they made the enlarged bill and paw appear still puzzles us."

Next, Zeghes heard Ytell scolding Alex, "I told you to go back to the entrance."

Alex, in an accusatory tone, responded, "You got rid of my bubble."

"I don't have time to figure out what's going on with you. Go stand by the wall."

Zeghes wanted to go play, but he wouldn't leave Alex. He could tell Alex wasn't happy, maybe even ill. Peter drifted through the air to Alex. "You're a lucky one, Alex. This evil has no grip on you." His voice rose. "I pray for my own release from this foul situation."

Alex stepped toward Peter. "But this is a chance for us to help other people."

"How can you trust what these aliens say? You're a child. How can you understand? I'm a preacher, a man of God. I know what's right and wrong."

Zeghes soared towards Alex and Peter. "Leave him alone! You sound like Heyeze. He led many of my people to their death. He tried to tell them he was the source of truth, but he knew nothing. He was evil. I don't know much, but claiming you know what's right and wrong is just like Heyeze."

"Ha," Peter said. "Animals don't have philosophers. You're lying."

Zeghes charged Peter's bubble and yelled, "Begone!" With a shriek that faded in the distance, Peter's bubble ricocheted about the hall.

A'idah came up to them. "Good job, Zeghes. The other humans need to respect everyone. Hang in there, Alex. We'll get this figured out."

As others gathered by Alex Ytell turned to Zeghes. "Zeghes, I understand why you attacked Peter, but we can't fight each other. Consider this your only warning. If you fight with each other, a device called a "civilization band" will be put on you. If you try to fight with the band on, it will knock you unconscious. Now everyone, head back to our common room. I'll meet you there."

"Ship, please give us a guide back to our rooms," Osama requested.

A ball of light materialized in front of the flock and bounced through the air toward the doorway they had come through earlier. Zeghes puzzled over Ytell's words as he followed the flock and listened to the conversations. He recalled fighting in the pod. Fighting was how everyone knew their place. What would everyone do if they didn't fight? If he learned how to fit in here, would he be able to fit in back in his pod? It was like the physical abduction was just the beginning of a process.

Osamu walked between A'idah and Alex. "Do not worry about the bubbles back there. These aliens will figure out what is wrong."

"This is an incredible place," Alex said, as he looked at Osamu. "I hope I don't get sent back to Earth."

Osamu patted Alex on the back. "I remember you telling us

Chapter 4

about saving the kittens. I know you react to Dark Matter. The aliens on this ship would not make a mistake."

"Maybe my saving the kittens was a one-time shot."

"Stop questioning yourself," Osamu said.

Starting to hobble, A'idah took Alex's hand. "It doesn't matter if you react to Dark Matter or not. It doesn't change who you are. They better not try to send you back. I'll refuse to stay. They can lock me up in a cage or torture me. It won't do them any good."

Zeghes nudged A'idah with his bill. "You're limping. We need to get you back to Gursha, so she can help you finish healing."

Skyler came flapping and dodging past them. "What a crazy flock this is. Flocks have to work together to survive. I need food. I'm so hungry."

Alex said, "A'idah, what's wrong? I thought you were cured."

"Gursha told me it will take a while for the nerves in my brain to fully heal. Until then, I have to put up with this whenever I do too much exercise."

As they arrived at their common room, two stocky people and one of the Kimley kids each pushing a cart loaded with food, came into the room from the other side. Zeghes hadn't realized how hungry he was until he saw a huge ball of water filled with fish floating behind the last cart.

One of the short men with a black beard said, "You're back just in time to eat. We're still having problems getting your food requirements all figured out. Another flock suffered food poisoning yesterday. Hopefully, no one else gets poisoned." He chuckled and pointed at his barrel chest. "I'm Numbel." He then pointed to a bald man with a pointed white beard. "The grumpy one over there's Haal, and our helper is Hhy. They will stay here to help with any problems."

A soft voice interjected, "Be careful with the fruit. I think someone goofed. It might be too spicy for you."

Zeghes looked over at the speaker. It was Hhy. He heard A'idah talking to Alex. "He's one of those troublesome Soaley boys. Come over here. How does this water float in the air?"

Zeghes turned his head to examine Hhy more closely with his sonar. But A'idah said Hhy was a...boy?

Osamu stood examining the big ball of water with fish swimming in it. Tentatively, he poked at it and waved his hands under it. "I would like to know too."

Alex said, "In the space station, doesn't water make balls like this?"

Osamu looked appraisingly at Alex. "Yes, Alex. What are you thinking?"

"Well," Alex said. "We're on a spaceship, and yet we're experiencing gravity. That means they must have technology to control gravity. I suspect they are making the area of the ball have no gravity."

"I knew you could tell me how the aliens did this," A'idah said.

Osamu raised one eyebrow. "Very good, Alex. I think you are right. Oh, the things we will do on Earth with this technology."

Zeghes feeling perplexed, hung in the air. What were they talking about? Ekbal's voice distracted him from continuing his thought.

"That fruit looks tempting to me," Ekbal said, hungrily. After gazing at it for a moment he walked over to the cart.

"Didn't you hear the fruit might be spicy?" Alex asked.

Ekbal paused, hand hovering over the fruit. "Yes, but the fruit looks so good." He took an orange and green-striped fruit and popped it into his mouth.

"Mmm this tastes good, not too hot." His face turned red, and tears streamed down his face. "Oh, hot! Water! Water!"

Hhy snatched both a pitcher and a glass off a cart and hurried toward Ekbal who with his tears blinding him, staggered about, waving his arms and calling for help.

Hhy ducked under one waving arm and dodged to the side. Ekbal blundered into the floating ball of water. Bubbles rose from his mouth as he tried to talk. Gasping and choking, he ducked back out of the water. Hhy poured Ekbal a drink and slipped a slender arm around him to support him. After Ekbal's breathing steadied, he took the glass and gulped the liquid down.

"Thanks," Ekbal said to Hhy. "You were right about your warning, but that fruit tasted wonderful. I wonder if a second one would be as painful."

As a dolphin, Zeghes had been considered curious, but he couldn't believe how curious Ekbal was. The rest of the flock mesmerized the young dolphin. He shifted his attention from one person to another. Sabu had retreated to a back corner, gnawing

Chapter 4

on something. Ekbal stood looking at the fruit and licking his lips. While everyone finished eating, Zeghes struggled with thoughts. Everyone else was fitting in and beginning to understand new things, but he was confused and just pretending to be comfortable with all of this.

As soon as Haal and Hhy started picking up after the meal, the flock jumped up, some to help, and some to eat a little more. Zeghes had only eaten a few fish. His thoughts and the flock members kept distracting him.

"Wait," Skyler said. "I want more nuts."

"You'll get too fat to fly," Sabu said and swatted playfully at Skyler's tail.

Skyler flapped away from him and knocked a bowl over, spilling its contents across the floor, as Ytell entered the room.

Seeing Ytell, Skyler said, "It was Sabu's fault. She swatted me."

Zeghes watched to see how Ytell would react. Ytell avoided looking at the bird. "Peter won't be coming back. Alex, come with me. We're going to Amable."

Zeghes looked back to Alex. He was his pod member and still sick. He didn't think the boy should go without him or A'idah, but how were sick people treated here?

"Alex, we need to go," Ytell said, impatiently.

Turning around, Alex acknowledged them leaving. "Bye."

Zeghes leaped through the air, bumping Alex with his head. "Will he not come back? Shouldn't one of us go with him?"

A'idah hobbled to Alex and took his hand.

Ytell said, "A'idah and Zeghes, on the world I grew up, your type of loyalty is greatly valued. Also, my world is a very harsh place. My people discard young who fail. Regardless of what the decision is, I will bring him back here. In the future, I need all of you to trust me. That will be hard for you. My training methods will often seem like you are on your own, but I'll be watching out for you. When we get to the academy, your training will be very dangerous at times. Part of the danger will be from what you are learning, and part of it will be from the need to hurry. I don't want you to fail. Remember, you are my flock, if need be, I would die for you."

"What?" Zeghes asked, as he looked around at the flock members for an answer. How could they discard their young?

Chapter Five
What will be done with Alex?

Meanwhile in Amable's office, Alex's fate was being discussed.

"No, no, no, we can't send Alex back to Earth," Amable said to Stick, a thin, six-foot-tall bald creature, the only other person in Amable's office. A faint tune, recognizable as *Ode of Remembrance,* could be heard emanating from the resting fish-plant.

Stick rubbed his chartreuse, bulbous forehead. "But he doesn't react to Dark Matter. He won't be able to do any types of vapuc. Keeping him for the next year is a waste of resources. Let me show you the figures."

"And I'm telling you, even if Alex doesn't react to Dark Matter, he'll be of use to the flock. If his flock develops as it should, they'll help deal with the threats to the academy. As a nonvapuc-able person Alex's life will be in danger, and his flock will have to learn to protect him," explained Amable. "That will be good for the flock, but I also hope we can find something Alex is good at."

"But sir, I checked with Gursha about Alex's sickness. She told me Alex isn't responding to treatment as he should. She doesn't think he'll recover from his illness. In fact, she suspects other aliens have done something to him. Alex could be part of Maleky's plan for Earth. It would be just the thing he would do."

"Of course, Stick," Amable replied. "And we can't forget the deception involved with Alex supposedly saving the kittens. He remembers saving the kittens, but he doesn't react to Dark Matter, except maybe sensing the future. Ergo, he couldn't have done vapuc in saving the kittens. Someone pulled off a difficult trick to convince our team he reacted to Dark Matter. Someone wanted us to find Alex."

"It has to be Maleky," Stick said, wiping sweat off his forehead.

Chapter 5

"What are we going to do about Alex? I still think we should send him back to Earth."

Amable placed his arm around Stick. "There is an old saying: keep your friends close and your enemies closer. We are keeping Alex very close."

"Then you won't use the two Soaley kids to test him?"

"I don't see why not," Amable said.

"But we don't trust them either."

"That's true," Amable said. "Having Alex and the kids together will let us keep an eye on all of them at the same time."

"Alex seems like such a nice boy," Stick said sadly. "Wouldn't it be better to send him back to Earth? Might we ... have to ... kill him?"

"You're letting your emotions get in the way of your logic. If Alex is a tool of Maleky, sending him back to Earth would be a death sentence. I'm surprised at you for suggesting killing Alex. We don't kill people unless it is unavoidable. Maleky destroys all of the tools that fail him. Besides, Mrs. Soaley took the rare action of sharing what she knew of the future, just to make sure we wouldn't miss Alex in our search of Earth for creatures that react to Dark Matter."

"We still trust the adult Kimleys?" Stick asked.

"Yes, as much as we trust anyone."

"Then we continue with your plan for Alex?"

"Yes."

~**********~

Still back with the flock, Alex held onto A'idah's hand. He didn't want to leave Zeghes, A'idah, and the others.

Zeghes glided right up to Ytell's beak. "I should go with Alex. He's still sick, and he might get abducted again."

Confused at his words, Alex looked at Zeghes. "How could I get abducted again?"

Zeghes hesitated and said, "Saying abduction was probably wrong. Our bodies were abducted the first time, but now, I feel like who I am is being abducted. I mean ... since I've been here, I've changed, and I'll never be the same again. My own self is being abducted. Who knows what these aliens will do to you?"

Ekbal came forward. "Wow, Zeghes. Dolphins do have philosophers"

A'idah said, "I think it's good to change. I'm looking forward to learning how to protect myself and others. But there's another type of abduction. Among my people, the Kalasha, I've seen older girls fall in love and get married. I think falling in love is a form of abduction, but Alex doesn't need to worry about it. How would he fall in love with an alien?"

Alex stood with his mouth open, as he tried to figure out what to say, but overwhelmed by his thoughts. Falling in love with an alien? Ew! that sounded gross and crazy! And why did Zeghes' concern about changing bother him?

Ytell reached a long, thin arm out from under his feathers to grasp Alex. "Okay, enough with all the talk. We have to go."

As Ytell pulled Alex after him, the group said their farewells.

"Good luck, Alex."

"If you see some nuts, get some."

"Remember to believe in yourself."

"Don't show fear. That's when the sharks attack."

Walking away from the flock, Alex tugged his arm away from the raptor. Ytell still felt quite alien to him, and feeling the scaly hand on his arm was unsettling. As they walked, he glanced at Ytell. "Would you really die for me?"

"Yes. For us raptors, it's a matter of honor."

"My Aunt Debbie died saving others. Dying so others can live is the greatest sacrifice."

"That's partly why Amable and all of us are fighting to save worlds from the deem. We are willing to give our lives for the battle."

After walking the nearly deserted halls with Ytell they stopped before a door. They heard a "Come on in," as the door slid open.

A strange man hurried over to Alex. His pink and violet hair had foot long tufts sticking out above his ears. He grasped Alex's hand and shook it vigorously. "Ah, here you are, Alex, a fine young man. I'm Amable, and the last time I saw you everyone was quite worried about you. I'm sorry we had to abduct you. We'd planned to recruit you students but ran out of time. We're in a hurry to get you back to our academy world. You know how important it is for

Chapter 5

us to get you trained. Then all of you students will be able to help save your own world. It's wonderful to see you looking better. Obviously, Gursha has worked her miracles on you. How're you feeling?"

Alex choked back a laugh, as he gazed at the strange-looking man with large golden-brown eyes set in a pale face. "Much better. It's been great getting healed. Gursha told me to come back again this—."

"She says you're doing great," Amable said, interrupting him. "She's going to check your progress, but she wants you to complete an exercise program. Your two personal trainers will meet you tomorrow. I'm so glad you've adjusted to being a student and for how willing you are for the important training. I presume you are willing to do this exercise program?"

Alex shrugged his shoulders. Trainers? What was he talking about? "I guess. What is it?"

"Just exercise," Amable said, subtly herding Alex and Ytell out of his office. "Glad you agreed to the program. The good news is you can rejoin your flock as soon as the training is over."

"Wait," Alex said. "Who are the trainers?"

"You'll meet them tomorrow," Amable said. "Goodbye."

And then the door shut in Alex's face. "Why wouldn't he answer me?" Alex asked Ytell.

Ytell squatted down to look Alex in the eye. "There's something he doesn't want to tell you. I'm sorry, but I don't know what it is."

Alex opened his mouth to respond then quickly shut it again. What could he say to the alien? How much were they not telling him or lying about? "I better go see Gursha."

Ytell nodded his head. "And I better get back to the rest of the flock. No telling what's going on there."

Alex stood alone in the passageway, as the sound of Ytell's footsteps faded. It was so quiet. Where was everyone?

Remembering the instructions for moving about in the halls he responded, quaveringly, "Ship, please supply a guide to Gursha's clinic."

A bright bobbing light floated in the air and moved opposite the direction Ytell took, and then waited for him. Alex shrugged trying to get rid of his nervousness. It didn't work.

Reluctantly, he started down the empty passageways toward

the clinic. At an intersection, he stopped. Did he hear a noise behind him? The light bobbed waiting. All Alex could hear was his heart. Walking faster, he resumed following the light. Minutes went by with one empty passageway after another. His heart beat louder and louder in the quietness.

A scream erupted from his mouth before he could stifle it. A strange misty green cloud had floated around the next corner. Alex stopped and quickly stepped back, warily watching the cloud. His guide light bounced to a halt.

"It's okay, Earthling," a feminine voice coming from the cloud said. "You don't need to be frightened."

"You didn't frighten me," Alex said lowering his hands and unclenching his fists. "I was just... startled."

The cloud girl floated along the passageway toward Alex. Holding his breath, he stepped to the side to let her pass. Just as the cloud drifted beside him she suddenly oozed through the air at him. With a gasp, Alex flattened himself against the wall. Warm, friendly laughter filled the air, and then abruptly stopped. The cloud girl swirled in the air to face down the passageway, the direction Alex had come. She backed up. A multitude of thoughts whirled in Alex's head. She was just teasing him. How could a cloud seem to face somewhere? He didn't see any eyes. A last thought made Alex both want to run and look down the passageway. What frightened her?

Alex looked down the hall to see a translucent creature roughly four feet wide and twice as tall. With its thick, trunk-like legs it stomped towards them. Each step caused shivers through its massive body.

In an urgent tone, the cloud girl said to Alex, "Go, go. I'll keep the baby Lepercaul from hurting you."

For a moment, Alex stood still. A baby? This was a baby?

The other creature spoke very strangely, with a voice both deep and threatening, yet oddly babyish. "I'm not a baby. And I just want to taste the Earthling. I've heard they're tasty. Ha-ha-ha," it laughed. "I wouldn't hurt him much. He-he-he-he."

Alex wanted to follow the cloud girl's advice, but concern for her held him back, "What about you?"

She moved past Alex and toward the threatening creature. Even more urgently she spoke to Alex, "Please, go. Hurry. I'll be

Chapter 5

okay. This monster can't really hurt me, but it could easily eat you. Go."

He started walking down the passageway, trying not to run from the strange and frightening situation. Everything was going to be okay. He wasn't scared. That thing could eat him??

Behind him, Alex heard the cloud creature trying to reason with the monster.

"You aren't supposed to be out here. You —"

"I can too. A Winkle has some fun for me."

Looking around with wide eyes, Alex walked faster and faster, until eventually, he ran gasping into the clinic.

Gursha's boisterous voice greeted him. "Hello, Alex. Is someone chasing you?"

Alex looked at her. He was going to be okay. He just needed to keep it together and not show how frightened he was. "No. I ... just didn't want to be late." Deep breath and change the conversation. "Where's all of your medical equipment?"

"The holo-fields are my equipment," Gursha said. "Less advanced technologies use a confusing amount of unsanitary medical tools. It's a wonder everyone in your hospitals doesn't die from infections. Now, lie down in this holo-field."

Alex smiled at Gursha and did as she asked. His view of the room turned pinkish as the haze of the holo-field surrounded him.

"Why am I seeing some things pinkish?" Alex asked.

"Pink haze shows the areas of illness or problems. That's what is coloring your view of the room. Now, I'm going back to my office and I want you to lie still."

Lying still, Alex started to think about the strange creatures he'd met in the halls. The situation couldn't have been as bad as it seemed. What was a Winkle? Alex closed the door on those thoughts. Everything was going to be okay. Next his thoughts wandered to Hhy. Something about the boy puzzled him. What was it? Then thoughts of A'idah crowded his mind. He understood A'idah. She was so .... He liked spending time with her. And then he laughed to himself. He was drawn to her because they were both human and she was a girl just a couple of years younger than him. He couldn't wait to see her again.

At that thought, he remembered his dad and a conversation they had back before his parents died. Anguish rose with the memory. "Son, you're becoming a teenager. You are going to have new feelings and urges. Eventually, you'll be drawn to girls. Be careful about letting the feelings and urges control you. You've seen the wonderful relationship your mom and I have. If you wait until you're older to get serious about a girl, then you can build a relationship like we have. Don't play with a girl's feelings. Treat her with respect. In your heart and mind, you'll know what's right. But it can be very difficult to do what's right. Know your mom and I'll always be there for you, and we'll be praying for you."

Except they weren't. Dad had lied. Tears started to flow down Alex's cheeks. He needed their help. He missed them.

At that moment, Gursha bustled in with Alex's dinner. "We're- Oh, Alex, what's wrong?" Gursha left the dinner to slip two hands under his shoulders, a third hand smoothed his hair back from his forehead, and the fourth hand held one of his hands.

Feeling like a baby, Alex leaned into Gursha. "I miss my folks."

"You'll see them in a year. We'll be taking you back for a visit."

"No. You don't understand. They're dead."

"Oh. Alex, it's good that you miss them. That means you love them. What do you believe about death?"

"My folks believed it was just a passage from this life to an eternal life."

Gursha looked into Alex's eyes. "What do you believe?"

"I don't know. When they died, I prayed to God, and I got comfort. But I don't really know what I believe."

"Alex, I've lost loved ones." Pausing to look away, Gursha added in a soft voice. "Too many." Taking a deep breath she looked back at Alex. "If you live life well, then you're going to lose people you care for, but if you never lived, then you never had them to lose. You have to find comfort in positive things that keep you living and giving. Be careful. There are things that will comfort, but they'll diminish you. The good kind of comfort keeps us strong in here." Gursha placed a hand over Alex's heart. "We have to be strong here to help those still living."

"Thanks, Gursha," Alex said.

"You can come to me with your problems anytime," Gursha said. "Now, we're making some progress with your cure. Your prescription is to eat, exercise, rest, and repeat."

"Repeat?" asked Alex.

Chapter 5

"Keep doing those three things until I tell you to stop," Gursha said.

"You mean when this is done, I won't have to eat or rest?"

"You know what I mean," Gursha said with a laugh. "Now eat this food, and get to sleep. Tomorrow will be a busy day for you."

"How long before I'm totally cured?"

The holo-field lifted Alex into a vertical position. Gursha then engulfed one of his hands with her large hand. "Alex, most of the fatigue is gone, but I'm having trouble getting rid of some problems. You and I will beat this. The uncertainty is part of the journey."

After Alex finished eating and as he drifted off to sleep, he heard her whispering to herself, "I hope Alex can defeat this evil inside him."

In the middle of the night, Alex's hands groped for a non-existent weapon. His eyes popped open, and he looked around Gursha's barren clinic in the dim light. A dream about battling evil inside him still felt so real. He remembered his disappointment the evening before, when Gursha told him he was going to have to fight the illness for a while longer. Trying to force himself to feel better, he daydreamed about Zeghes and A'idah giving him his training. All the time, he wanted and hoped to fall back asleep and have better dreams. His worry about the illness morphed into wondering who or what would be training him. He didn't know any of the aliens, and he couldn't imagine understanding just how strange some of them were.

Finally, his body relaxed, and he drifted back off to sleep. In the morning, Alex's eyelids fluttered in his deep sleep. A smile tugged at his mouth from the dream. A flowery fragrance drifted about on a breeze blowing across a meadow filled with strange and yet beautiful plants. A tall figure stepped out of dark evergreens bordering the meadow and walked slowly toward him. She wore a brown robe and her long light-brown hair danced in the breeze. Streaks of gold and red hair twinkled in the sunlight. She raised her face, and he saw dark eyes with long curly eyelashes. Leisurely, she swayed closer to him. The red of her lips caught his attention as the full lips slowly curved into a smile. Alex's heart began to beat faster, and he stepped forward.

She demurely ducked her head to the side. A slender hand covered the smile, but Alex could tell she still smiled because of two dimples in her cheek. He felt the desire to brush his fingers lightly across the cheek and then trace the jawline back to the firm chin and touch her lips. How exotic she was. His breath came faster. Her jaw shouldn't be so long. Alex froze and took a quick step back.

The girl dropped her hands and turned a pleading face toward him. Her eyes were too big to be normal. She lifted her hands and the robe slipped over her skin to show long graceful arms. "Don't be afraid. I love you." She paused, mouth slightly open, and Alex could see her sharp pointed teeth. She was an alien. He tried to scream, but nothing would come out. He tried to turn and run, except he'd lost all control of his body. He grew more and more terrified as he watched her come closer. She lifted one hand to the side of his face. He felt it playing in his hair. In a sultry voice she whispered in his ear. "It won't hurt you, too much."

She slipped back and he watched her lips pucker for a kiss and felt his own responding for the contact. He wanted to kiss her. Then he was awake and gasping in the holo-field. "No. No. No. Gross. I do not want to kiss an alien."

~**********~

The previous day a teenage girl - a woman almost - hurried through the corridors. She had the slight build and features of Earth's fabled elves. The top of her pointed ears stuck up out of her shoulder length, white hair. She blinked her large violet eyes when she saw her Father ahead of her and slowed to his pace. He stopped at the door to the Weird room and she stopped with him. Slowly and hesitantly she approached, remembering what was hanging in her room's closet and the note her father had left for her. It had read, "Hheilea, this is your time. You need to begin preparations. Amable has given me permission to use the Weird room. Meet me there."

Her father turned toward her, not looking directly at her. She heard her father answer her future question, "I cannot tell you who it will be. The *t'wasn't-to-be-is* ceremony will give you that answer."

Hheilea stood still gritting her teeth. She hated being a Kimley. She had to pretend to be a boy, and look like a kid instead of the young woman, which she was. Still, she could be abducted anytime. No one else could ever understand how terrible and dangerous her life was. Her father couldn't see her smile at him. Instead, he saw the future. He tried to talk to her, but he was talking to her possible future. His subconsciousness lived in '*now*', but what good did that do her? Hheilea looked at her father, her mouth firmly shut refusing to ask the question he had already answered even as she heard it in her mind. *Who would he be?* Her older cousin had been the only possibility she knew of, but he'd been kidnapped.

Beads of Sweat stood out on her father's forehead. "For your sake and the sake of what's coming, I'm trying to get as close to *now* as I can."

Excitement tried to bubble up in Hheilea, but her fear tamped it down, even as she thought the t'wasn't-to-be-is must be drawing her future husband toward her. A young Kimley man must be traveling to the academy or might be there already. What would her future husband look like? Her father's difficulty spoke of why she didn't want to be an adult. Once she matured, she would never live again in *now* like all other creatures. She'd be another oddity, just someone to kidnap and torture in order to get answers about the future. She didn't want to live in the future like her parents. Again her father spoke. "I'll wait for you inside." And then he entered the doorway.

He knew Hheilea didn't want to do this and would put off entering. Fighting against her fears and wanting to go against the future he saw, she rushed after him. Her emotions shook her body as they stood in a featureless, white room.

Her father faced her, but wasn't quite looking at her. A grin covered his face. "The future probability showed you not coming in for a long time, but knowing my daughter's strength of will, I suspect you fought your natural inclination and came in right behind me. I also expect you to be pretty upset. I was too, at this time of my life. We've come to the Weird room because of what you're going to do. I know the artificial intelligence controlling this room and have talked to him. This is the safest place on our spaceship. Here, your subconsciousness will be safe taking care of your body for the first time."

Hheilea wanted to grin back, and she wanted to slug him. Tears of frustration rolled down her cheeks and she swung at him, knowing his subconscious would see and block the blows. Briefly, they sparred until she stopped gasping for breath.

Her father held out a hand with a vial. "Take this, drink it, and hold my hands."

Hheilea stood for a long time looking at the vial. What was it? Was this the beginning of the end of being conscious of her surroundings? Finally, she took it, opened the vial, and drank it all in one gulp. The liquid burned down her throat, leaving her gasping. Hheilea desperately lunged for his hands, as vertigo temporarily made her dizzy. The room around her faded away leaving Hheilea standing with her father on the gray, gently, shifting ground. Around them were colors like shifting panes of colored glass hanging in the air.

She started to drop to the ground, overwhelmed by the experience, but strong arms caught her, holding her up. "Oh my daughter, how I have looked forward to this."

Those words didn't sound right to Hheilea. It sounded as if he was in the *now* or maybe (and she gulped at the thought) she was in the future with him. She looked up to gaze into his eyes.

He winked at her and said, "This is going to feel very strange for you, but you'll be traveling as a Kimley adult, even though you're still a child, through the dimensions of time and space for the first time. Come on. Our family's anxious to see you."

He reached toward a green pane, and his hand disappeared into the color. It was followed by his arm, and his body streamed into the green pane.

Eyes wide in wonder, Hheilea's hand held by her father and then her whole body entered the color after him. For just a moment green surrounded her. She was traveling as an adult through time's dimensions. The green color faded away and now she stood in a different place. A group of people crowded forward. Hheilea backed into her father and gasped. She recognized her grandparents, but they were dead. How could they be here? And who were all of the others?

Her dad said, "Everyone, here's Hheilea."

She stepped forward and briefly hugged her grandparents long separated from her, but confusion made her stop, pull back, and look around. "How are you all here?"

Many different voices spoke at once. One of the ladies she didn't recognize shouted, "Quiet!" She continued in a lower volume. "Hello, dear. I'm your great-great-great-grandma. In your bewilderment, you've forgotten what your lessons have taught you. Our consciousness lives in the future and travels through time. Remember dear, for us time isn't a dimension as most creatures treat it. Time itself has dimensions. We're all in time. I came from your past to this location in time to see you."

Another vaguely familiar lady came up to her. "Let me hold you."

Hheilea held both hands up to ward off the stranger and stepped back. Her eyes filled, and tears threatened to fall. She remembered the lessons taught at home in the dining room. Anger and frustration pushed away the perplexity. Questions bubbled up in her. Her voice cracking with emotion, she asked them, pleading for an answer. "Why?" she cried. "Why, if we are so powerful? We can see into the future and travel through time. Why have we let our people get captured and sold into slavery?"

Everyone stepped aside, and an old man stepped forward. "Hello, Hheilea. Small things are easy to avoid, but each choice makes a new future. There is one big danger looming in the future with only one possible way to defeat it. We choose the path of hope for everyone's future. You may have heard the saying 'With great power comes great responsibility.' It also comes with many painful choices."

Her father nodded at the words, "Sorry, everyone, but you all know about a Kimley's first time to travel as an adult. Her time with us is up. I must take her back to her body. Goodbye. Come with me Hheilea."

Taking her hand, he reached for a red pane. With her free hand, she waved goodbye to all the family members. They disappeared as her hand and then her body flowed into the red pane. Briefly, all she could see was red. Then again, she stood alone with her father back on the first, gray landscape and she asked, "What did the old man mean?"

Her father looked at her. "Being able to see possible futures doesn't make us all powerful. Sometimes pain and suffering is the only way to get to the best future. We have to make difficult choices." He hugged her. "Be brave."

Again, the tears flowed. "Why haven't you done this before, Daddy?"

He sighed as he looked back at her. "The potion in the vial only works when you're beginning into the t'wasn't-to-be-is. Your subconscious has noticed the beginning changes for your t'wasn't-to-be-is ceremony. But you'll still be confused and puzzled until the ceremony begins in earnest. All children get this experience at your age. Soon you'll no longer be a child. This experience showed you what it's like to be an adult Kimley and will encourage you not to fight against the changes happening to you. When the moment is right, you'll know your time as a child is at an end. When that time comes to pass, the t'wasn't-to-be-is plant will bear fruit, and you'll begin the dance to become one with your life partner. Your time here is done. You're returning to *now*. I love you."

They were back in the Weird room, and her father wasn't quite looking at her.

Chapter Six
Hheilea

In the morning, Hheilea and her brother, Hymeron, ran through the passageways. Hymeron, a good eight inches shorter than Hheilea, was obviously younger. They both wore baggy, gray pantaloons with colorful vests.

Hymeron laughed and said, "I'm looking forward to having him in our control. Remember you agreed to do what I want."

Hheilea didn't say anything. Troubled thoughts bothered her as they drew near to the clinic. This human had been part of why Mom was sick. It was Mom's choice, but this human's existence caused the problem. She nodded and said, "Yes, he's going to pay."

Light-footed, they dodged around other aliens in the passageways. Hheilea slowed as they came near the clinic. Hymeron snickered.

Stick, with a holographic display of pictures and text surrounding him, entered the clinic ahead of them. The holograph itself was transparent. As he walked, he waved his hands through the air. In response, the information around him changed, and one picture brought a chuckle from him.

Hymeron gave a hand signal to Hheilea. Meanwhile, voices came from the clinic. Ignoring the voices, the two of them snuck into the room behind Stick and tripped him. Immediately, they ran back into the passageway, laughing quietly. Behind them, Hheilea heard the crash of the man falling, followed by someone laughing.

Stick wailed. "No!"

Hheilea came to a stop with her brother. Regret extinguished her laughter. The next moment, a hand grasped her shoulder, and she saw Hymeron caught by another hand. Amable frowned down at them and dragged them into the clinic. "Are you all right, Stick?"

In the clinic, Alex and Gursha finished helping Stick to his feet.

At first, Stick didn't answer. He let Gursha hold his face against hers as she whispered to him, and then pushed away from her to face Amable, "No. I'm not alright. I just lost months of paperwork, thanks to those two troublemakers."

"Months?" Amable asked, raising a single bushy eyebrow.

"Okay, days," Stick said. "But still, I thought you were going to do something about them terrorizing me."

"I'm giving Hhy and Hymeron a job right now. Also, if I hear of them causing more problems they will be confined to their quarters."

"Great, just great. If Alex's training must go forward, I'll take my contrary opinion to tech support and try to get my files recovered."

Amable said, "Go ahead and good luck."

Before Stick left, Alex spoke up. "Your nose—it's blue."

"Of course, it's blue," sputtered Stick. "Whenever it gets hurt, it turns blue. That's normal."

Amable looked down at Hheilea and Hymeron. "This is Alex. Remember what I told you about behaving." Amable looked back up and said to Alex, "Hhy and Hymeron are your trainers."

Alex looked after the departing Stick, not paying attention.

"Alex, did you hear me?" Amable asked. "These two boys, Hhy and Hymeron, are going to give you training and exercise."

"What?!" Alex stepped back, accidently activating a holo-field. Alex screamed as he was lifted up into the air and the two Kimleys laughed as he waved his arms and legs about in a comical struggle. He cut the scream off and glared at them. Breathing deeply, he turned a pleading look at Amable. "I'm still trying to get used to being in an alien place, with strange creatures, and you're going to stick me with them?"

"Yes, Hymeron and Hhy Soaley. They're brothers."

Hheilea grinned at his consternation, not noticing the quiet notes of a song in her head. Life would be so much easier if she didn't have to hide and act like a boy. And she didn't like being called Hhy.

Her brother said, "You're funny. Could you wave your arms and legs about again?"

Sounding desperate, Alex said, "But they're just little kids."

Hheilea stood up straight and stomped up to Alex, tipping her head to look him in the eyes as she did. The top of her head came up just short of Alex's chin. "I'm not that much shorter than you, you big lump, so don't call me a little kid."

"Have fun. I'll see you later." Amable's ear tufts gently waving, he made his escape from the room.

"Wait! Come back! Don't leave me with them."

Hymeron laughed and said, "If you're done eating, let's go."

Alex checked his shoes before looking at the Kimleys. Hheilea looked back at him. She wondered how old he was. He was the kid, not her.

Alex opened his mouth, hesitated, and asked, "Where are we going?"

"To give you some exercise," Hheilea said. She ignored the distant sounds of music in her head and walked away with a laugh.

As Alex walked with them down the hall, Hheilea thought back to her experience with her dad. Vaguely, she heard Hymeron talking to Alex.

Then Alex screamed, "Aaah!"

Hheilea stopped and looked back. Alex stood looking down a passageway, talking to himself.

"A huge spider, I'm going to be frightened. I don't want to be frightened. Wait, I'm not really frightened, just a bit scared." Alex continued talking to himself, but too quietly for her to hear.

This human boy was crazy. Hheilea turned to her brother to see what he thought. Her brother had a disappointed look on his face.

Hymeron told her. "Earlier Gursha told me, via my AI, that she would give him a drug forcing him to face his fears and analyze how he felt. I thought he would be crying and screaming for help."

His expression changed to a hopeful look and he added. "At least the special experience I've prepared should be fun."

The second time Hymeron stopped, she waited trying not to think about what Hymeron was doing to the human. A flowery fragrance caught her attention. Was there a nasty Winkle around? A quiet voice made her look back at the human. Alex stood, lips puckered, and a Winkle girl leaned seductively against him. Hheilea gasped, feeling warmth in her cheeks. A thought blazed across her mind. What was that minx doing? She better not.... Hheilea turned on her brother and slugged him. "What are you doing working with a Winkle? You know how cruel they are."

Hymeron stepped away from her. "Get a grip on yourself. I'm just having some fun."

Hheilea warred with the ideas of strangling her brother or running over to tackle the Winkle. At a gasp of pain from Alex, Hheilea whirled around. The human stood against the wall blood dripping from his chin. Her brother had gone too far. This was wrong. A young Lepercaul, four feet wide and twice as tall, thundered down the hall and attacked Alex. Hheilea lost all restraint. Her brother grabbed her as she growled and started to go to Alex's aid. She didn't have any plans for what to do against the monstrous creature. She wasn't thinking, just reacting. Hheilea fought him until help in the form of Alex's flock leader showed up.

Ytell hollered from the other end of the hall. "Enough! Leave my flock member alone!"

The Winkle and the Lepercaul ran back through the doorway they had come from. Ytell ruffled his feathers and in a very upset tone exclaimed, "Hymeron, you do not want to be in trouble with me! Take Alex to the Weird room! Now!"

Her brother spoke in the petulant tone she hated. "Okay don't get your feathers all fluffed up. I was going to stop it... before they hurt him..., much. Come on, Alex."

In a quieter voice he added to Hheilea. "I wasn't letting them hurt Alex, just roughing him up a bit. It's good training for him. He needed to see the reality of his situation. You and I knew this would be a dangerous situation for everyone, but Alex didn't. Now he does."

Behind them, Alex walked at an increasingly slower pace. Then he spoke with anger in his voice. "Isn't that the same door we went past earlier? At this rate, when I arrive at wherever you're dragging me, I'll be too tired to exercise."

"It's only been about thirty minutes," Hheilea answered. "Although he's right. We should stop going in circles and get him to the Weird room."

Hymeron looked at both of them. "Oka—"

The door opened and a familiar translucent head looked out into the hall. The creature spoke in a babyish and yet strangely deep voice, interrupting Hymeron. "Hi. Humans do taste good."

Hymeron said, "Where's Twarbie? She was supposed to take you back to your wild space."

The baby laughed. "I told her to take me back. She leaned against the wall and said, 'I like that boy.' Then, I thought about Human. I wanted to eat him."

Everyone stood still for a second. Then Hymeron said, "Your job's over and you're supposed to return to your wild space."

"Don't want to," Whined the baby Lepercaul. Then, in a deeper, much more confident tone, declared, "I'm going to eat Human."

Hymeron retreated a step. Blusteringly, he said "You can't do that."

Hheilea considered the conversation even as she whispered to Alex. "Start walking away." Why did she have a brother? Boys were such a pain. The Winkle likes Alex? She didn't believe it. Hheilea stepped toward the baby even as Hymeron backed up. In a calm voice, she said, "If you try to eat the human, your parents will be mad at you and take away your favorite foods."

The baby reached a giant hand toward Hheilea. She flinched, but stood still. "You don't—"

The baby spoke over her voice. "Parents don't care about others. How do you taste?"

In a surprisingly fast move the Lepercaul lunged at Hheilea, but she ducked. The Lepercaul's arm still slapped against her head. Burning pain ripped across her skull and white hair drifted toward the floor. The floor seemed to rise to meet her, but she twisted and caught herself with one hand. Spinning, she slammed the other hand down.

She looked up from her awkward position to see the baby laugh at her as he swiped at her midriff with a massive hand. Hheilea dropped to her back and rolled. All the time, she expected to feel pain explode and the blow connect, pinning her to the floor. Instead, there was just a tug on her vest. A trickle of pain down her back accompanied the tug on her clothes. Frantic, Hheilea continued the roll back to her feet. She thrust against the ground and sprinted, screaming, "Run!"

Alex responded to her command by shutting his mouth and turning to run away. Hymeron sprinted past Alex. "Follow me. He can't run as fast as us. We'll get away."

Hheilea ignored her vest flapping loose on her arms. However, she couldn't ignore the unfamiliar freedom from the binding. Her chest bobbed and swung with each step she took. Anger and pain filled her voice as she yelled at Hymeron. "Call Ytell about the wild baby."

Hymeron yelled back. "I got ahold of Twarbie, the Winkle. She's supposed to return the baby to its wild."

Too quickly, Hheilea caught up with Alex. If they survived, she'd strangle her brother. This human better not see … She held an arm against her chest. Behind her, the thudding of the baby's running interrupted her thoughts. "Can't you go faster?" She half asked and half demanded of Alex.

Alex shook his head and gasped. "No… too… tired."

Hheilea wanted to scream. She moved up beside him and shouted at Hymeron. "We need another plan! The baby's going to catch us!"

The human said, "Leave…"

"Go faster," Hymeron shouted back.

"me…"

"Alex can't!"

"behind."

"I'll open a Utility portal!"

A swirling pattern formed quickly on the wall, widening to reveal a large hole. Hymeron dove through it. "Hurry up," he called out to Alex and Hhy. "Hopefully he's too big to follow us."

The thumping footsteps drew nearer every second. Fear and the memory of the pain from the Lepercaul pushed Hheilea to go faster. Instead, she slipped an arm behind Alex and gripped the top of his pantaloons. She dove, jerking him after her. Her arm twisted

Chapter 6

and she felt her hand slip loose. Would Alex make it to safety? She was through the hole and tumbling. The weight of another body slammed into her. Together, they tumbled to a stop with Alex pinning her, face down. "Get off me, you big lump."

She felt his hand on her back shoving her harder into the floor. "Hey!"

Hymeron said, "Hurry up, you two. The baby's trying to get through the hole."

The weight shifted. Bitterly, she thought of where that hand would be if she'd landed on her back. At least she was on her stomach. She was so looking forward to being done with this human. She scrambled up to her knees and crawled away from the hole. Her blouse hung loose in front of her. Great. Just great. Why didn't she just rip it all the way off and make sure everyone found out she was a girl. Then she could stop hiding and face her doom.

Voices spoke in the dim light

"Hey, watch where you're going."

"What are you doing in here?"

Snakelike creatures slithered on the floor.

Alex gasped out an apology. "Sorry…. The back… of your clothes… are ripped… and I think you're bleeding."

Standing up Hheilea looked back. She saw Alex against the light from the hole. Good thing guys were so dumb or he might notice she was a girl. "Don't look at me," she stated, furiously. "Keep moving. It can reach through the hole. You're too close to the opening." Clenching her teeth, she tucked her blouse into her pantaloons.

A big thump, followed by a whining voice signaled the baby's attempt to get through the portal. "Stop running, I'm hungry." There was a brief pause, before they heard, "Oh! I could eat these things!"

Alex stopped to look back. "What are they?"

Flashes of light from behind them lit up the dim passageway. She doubted the baby would like getting shocked. Hheilea caught up to him and tugged on his arm. "Come on. We've got to keep going. The Zorms won't distract it for long. They're more mechanical than flesh and won't let the baby eat them. They've been exploring the ship since the slaves rebelled against the ship's original owners, the Deems. They also help with the ship's maintenance."

Movement to the side caught her vision. Reflections. Crystals leaned against the wall. Sounds of the fight faded as they moved on.

Hheilea said, "Be careful. We don't want to break these crystals. Deems are the only ones who know how to grow some of them."

Both of them slowed. A colorful, pulsating glow came from around a corner. They walked around the bend and stopped. Hheilea gazed in wonder. Instead of a passageway there was a crystal forest. Each crystal pulsed and coruscated with different colors. Hymeron waved. "Come on."

Carefully they walked into the forest. More of the snakes slithered about. Alex reached out to touch a crystal and Hheilea slapped his hand away. "Don't touch them."

Alex said, "They look alive."

Hymeron said, "They are. We're in a secret garden. I've helped the Zorms procure some things for their experiments. So they're okay with us being here, but don't tell anyone else about this. They hold grudges, and you don't want to find out how they get even. If we damaged these crystals, I'd have to either do what they said or suffer the consequences."

"Uh, oh," Hhelia said.

A familiar thumping sound grew louder. Hheilea grabbed Alex by the hand again. "Run."

Hymeron shouted. "Come on you two! We've gotta get out of here!"

Hheilea wrapped a strong arm around Alex's back and supported him as they continued on. "It's no use. We can't outrun

Chapter 6

it. This time you've really gotten us into bad trouble, Hymeron. You need to call Ytell or Amable for help."

"No, we can't call them from here." Hymeron's words snapped out of him. "This'll work. When this portal opens, get through it quickly. It won't stay open long. Don't wait or you could get stuck in it. Just don't break any crystals."

A shimmering in the air caught Hheilea's attention. In a second the shimmering spread in a circle, leaving a view of the normal hall in the middle.

"Jump!"

Hheilea jumped, pulling at Alex as she went, then found herself tumbling on the passageway floor. What was that snapping sound? This time she shoved away from Alex, trying to keep her clothing covering her front. She didn't wait for him or help him, but leapt to her feet. Hymeron was already standing by the Weird room door. She moved to join him.

From behind her, she heard Alex ask, "Where's the baby?"

Hymeron said, "The baby? You mean the terror. If it didn't break any crystals, Twarbie will find it and get it back to its wild. If not... well... the Zorms will take care of it."

Hheilea opened the door and entered. The room was empty and completely white. She remembered her brother's plans and slumped against the wall. She didn't like what would happen to this poor clueless human. "Hymeron, use your AI to talk to the Weird about healing my AI and me. Also, I need some new clothes."

Immediately her ripped blouse was replaced by a new one, and she felt the familiar binding of a vest. "Never mind, the Weird room heard me without my AI working." She looked up to see Alex standing in front of her.

"Back there, a couple of times, you risked your life to save mine. Thanks."

Hymeron said to Alex, "Hey, I saved your life with those portals, and don't tell anyone about them. If you have any energy left, start your training."

Alex looked around. "Uh, there's nothing in here."

Hymeron pointed at Alex. "Start running, unless you're wimped out."

"Where to?"

"That wall."

"Ha. The wall. Right." Alex took a couple of strides but didn't reach the wall. Hheilea watched Alex's expression and laughed at his surprise.

"What's going on?" Alex asked in amazement as he started to run.

Alex stopped after few seconds. With his hands on his knees, he asked between pants, "Why do I ... never get ... closer ... to the wall?"

"This is a special place in many ways," Hymeron said. "The room's called the Weird, but more importantly that's the name of the artificial intelligence running this room. You're going to stay in this room until your training is done. The Weird will provide everything you need until you leave. Look at what he did for us."

Hheilea, holding a tall, cold drink, relaxed in a chair. She could see a little bit of the holo-field the Weird had around her head as it healed her and her AI. The feeling of her hair growing back made her want to find a mirror. A variety of snacks covered a small table between her and where Hymeron himself rested in another chair.

Alex turned around and stared, open-mouthed, at them. "Where did all of that come from?"

"The same place as that chair," Hymeron said, snickering at the expression of surprise on Alex's face. Another chair appeared beside theirs.

"The Weird changes reality as easily as you change your clothes. Speaking of which, sweaty as you are, I bet instead of a chair you'd enjoy a shower," Hheilea said, grinning. Having the Weird do things to this unsuspecting boy was fun.

"That would feel good. Where is it?" Alex looked around and then said to Hheilea. "What are you grinning about?"

Hheilea almost laughed out loud as the first drop of water hit Alex, who looked up at a small, dark cloud. Rain poured down onto the boy's upturned face. Stumbling, Alex tried to get away, but it followed him. Then he headed toward Hheilea with a determined look, and her eyes grew wide as she realized his plan. She quickly

Chapter 6

asked the Weird to stop the rain.

"Great, guys. Now how about some dry clothes?" Alex asked, laughing.

Giggling, they pointed to a new door. Alex cautiously approached the door. He returned in moments wearing dry clothes.

After lunch and a nap for Alex, Hheilea and Hymeron took turns setting Alex up for pranks. She liked how easy going he was and tried to make her pranks something he might laugh at, but Hymeron took enjoyment in increasingly mean tricks. Last was another run at the wall, except this time, Alex ran into the wall and crumpled onto the floor, moaning in pain.

Hheilea stood and started to go to Alex, but Hymeron caught her by the arm and whispered fiercely at her. "Don't interfere. You promised to do what I want."

Hheilea glared at him and jerked her arm free.

Alex interrupted their argument by getting slowly to his feet. Panting and in obvious pain, he spoke in an accusatory tone. "You guys knew that was going to happen. I've had it."

Panting and weaving, Alex chased the kids until the floor turned slippery, his feet went out from under him, and he crashed limply onto the floor. A large, soft pillow appeared under his head just before he landed. In a second, he had fallen asleep.

Immediately, Hheilea turned and stormed across the floor at Hymeron. She jabbed a finger at him as he backed up until he fell. She spoke quietly but fiercely, not wanting to wake Alex. "You're being cruel. Sure, we're both upset about most of our people being slaves, but it really isn't everyone's fault. Amable and all the others we live with are trying to keep us safe. In the past, it felt good to do pranks, but at some point we have to grow up."

Hymeron said, "But he's the cause of Mom getting sick."

IIheilea swung her arm to point back at Alex. "This boy had nothing to do with Mom's decision."

Her ferocity shut up Hymeron. Immediately after saying, 'Mom's decision', Hheilea remembered the words of the old Kimley man, 'You may have heard the saying with great power comes great responsibility. It also comes with many painful choices.' She said, "I was with Mom. Her Cadley told Amable's team where to look for Alex. Mom knew the cost. Her act must have been important." And as she spoke, her own symbiotic Cadley, a little green lizard-like creature with large, bright eyes, peeked out of her hair.

"It isn't fair that Mom's sick," Hymeron said.

Hheilea scowled. The fact that sharing information about the future can make an adult Kimley sick irritated her and scared her, which irritated her more. "Of course, it isn't fair. Life isn't fair, but that doesn't mean we have to be horrible. Let's talk to him."

After a long pause, Hymeron said, "Ok."

She turned from her brother and headed for a door. "The Weird will let us know when he's waking up."

The door led to another area still within the Weird where they had everything they would need for the next months of the training. Hheilea was surprised at how much time passed before the Weird informed her Alex was waking up. They really had worked him too hard. Walking toward Alex, she smelled something flowery. "What's that scent?"

Hymeron asked, "What scent?"

It was gone. Hheilea wasn't sure if she'd imagined it. For a moment, she'd thought a Winkle was there. Using her AI she sent a question to the Weird. |Weird, where did the flower scent come from?|

She heard the response in her head. |Flower scent? What flowery scent? Maybe Alex knows.|

Hheilea snorted to herself. The human was clueless about what was going on. It must have been a strange joke the Weird was playing. She'd just ignore it. She said to Hymeron, "Remember what I said. We're going to treat him better."

Hymeron said, "I wasn't that hard on him. I still think you're overreacting because you're a g—."

"Hush," Hheilea hissed. "He might be awake."

Walking back to Alex, she nudged him. "Alex, wake up."

"What?" Alex asked, rolling over.

"We'll have a snack and talk about your training," she said.

Alex said, "I'm too sore to eat."

"Okay," Hheilea said and had the Weird increase the smell of the food.

Alex sat up. "What are you guys eating?"

"Here's a bowl for you," Hymeron said.

Alex eagerly reached for the bowl and then paused, looking

intently into Hymeron's face, "Is it safe for me to eat?"

Hheilea snatched the bowl from Hymeron and grasped a spoon that materialized in midair. She stirred the contents of the bowl and took a bite. After swallowing, she said, "It's a little spicy, but safe."

Finally, Alex took the offered food, shoveled some into his mouth, and mumbled his thanks. Hheilea looked at the bruises forming on Alex's face. Even though they had been caused by her brother's pranks, she felt responsible. "How's your face?"

"Sore." Alex said, and after he swallowed, he continued. "What's with you two? Do you have to do so many stupid things?"

In a petulant voice, Hymeron said, "But we didn't do hardly anything."

Alex glared back. "The small rainstorm was kind of funny. Making small, round rocks fly at me hurt. The pit that opened up in the floor scraped my legs pretty bad." Pointing at his bruised face and cuts on his arm, Alex added, "That doesn't cover the crazy time I had just getting to this room. I can go on."

"I thought it was funny," Hymeron said.

Alex pointed at his bruises and cuts. "Look at my face. Does that look funny?"

Hymeron glared back at Alex and then looked down at the floor.

When Alex turned to glare at Hheilea, the tinkling notes of a wind chime softly played in her head, growing stronger. Hheilea still refused to acknowledge the music. "I'm sorry, I got a little carried away with some of the pranks. I never wanted you to get hurt, but you can't understand what it's like being a Kimley."

"A little?" Alex asked with a bitter laugh. "I don't care about your problems. They still don't give you an excuse to torture me or mistreat others."

"We—I didn't mean to hurt you," Hhcilca said. "Thc Wcird has controls to prevent anyone from dying, and it can heal you. I'm surprised he didn't heal you already. Maybe it wanted to keep the evidence. Weird, please heal Alex."

A holo-field formed around Alex.

"Why are you caving in?" Hymeron asked Hheilea. Looking at Alex, he added, "And why do you have to be such a good sport about Hhy's pranks? You actually laughed at some of the things he did."

Red-faced, Hymeron stepped closer to Alex. "Hhy's behaving like a wimp, and I'm not surprised. Hhy's—." He stopped speaking and ground his teeth.

Alex shoved his face close to Hymeron's. "Hhy's what?"

Hheilea jabbed her brother in the ribs. The idiot, he almost told her secret.

Hymeron clutched his side and looked at Hheilea. "I'm sorry. The worst of what happened was my fault."

Alex stared at the two of them. "Okay, but do you two remember Amable's threat of confining you to quarters? If you go back to doing stupid pranks, Amable will hear about it."

"That's fair," Hheilea said. She turned away from them and spoke over her shoulder. "Race you to the top of the hill."

"What hill?" Alex asked.

Hheilea laughed, as a warm breeze brought the smell of salt water to her, and grass waved on the slope of a hill in front of them. Warmth on her skin made her look up. Instead of a ceiling, a violet sky with puffy, white clouds and two suns - one dull-red and the other yellow - met her eyes. She recognized them. From the bottom of the hill, she heard Alex ask, "What happened? Where are we?"

Hymeron said, "This is still the same room. Don't ask us how the Weird does this. We don't have a clue."

From the top of the hill, Hheilea watched Alex collapse on the ground from the effort of keeping up with her brother. He doesn't know how to give up. If Hymeron would behave, they could have fun. She still ignored the music, which, like the sound of approaching waves, grew in volume as she watched Alex.

Chapter Seven
Practice

One evening, weeks later, the two suns had set, and clusters of bright stars started appearing in the sky. Hheilea sat by a fire, picking at her dinner. At first she had liked being on this simulation of her people's home planet, but it had become too much.

Her friend, Alex, interrupted her attempt at getting the Weird to change the scene. "Wow, what a sunset! Or was it a suns-set?"

Hheilea quietly said, "This is the view from our home planet."

"Hhy, I bet you love it there," Alex said. Hheilea didn't say anything. "What's wrong?"

Hheilea frowned at her friend. She didn't want to be there … It hurt to be reminded …, and she didn't want him learning about … He'd pity her. "You aren't pronouncing my name right. It's Hhy, not Hi."

"I'm sorry, H*hy*." Alex said and then reached toward Hheilea. "Why the sad face?"

Hheilea watched his hand moving toward her. She wanted him to comfort her and understand. Sighing, she said, "We've never been to our home world. No Kimley lives there anymore. I wish we weren't reminded of it."

"What happened?"

Hheilea bit her lip. Why did her friend have to keep asking questions? It hurt to talk about it. Couldn't he see her pain? "Our people were attacked…and sold into slavery."

"That's terrible."

She shrugged. It was worse than terrible for her. "It isn't as bad now. Some of us have been freed."

Hheilea begged the Weird to change the scene and give them something to do. All of a sudden the stars were gone and three game controllers appeared next to Hheilea. With a sigh of relief she reached for one of them. "Let's play some games."

"Wait," Alex said. "If your home world makes you sad, why did you have the Weird make it seem like we were in your home world?"

Hymeron scowled. "We didn't. The Weird decides the scenes. We can ask for things and make suggestions, but it's in control."

Surprised, Alex looked at Hheilea. She nodded in agreement. Alex said, "But, weren't you boys controlling my training?"

Hheilea stood up. He was an idiot. Couldn't he see she wasn't a boy? And she wasn't a kid. Tears threatened to spill from her eyes. "We're just two kids good at playing pranks and games. The Weird doesn't need us for your training. Right now it looks like we should play some games."

"No, the Weird can wait," Alex said.

The ground shook, and a rumble filled the air. Hheilea thought to the Weird. |Thanks for having us play games.| With a relieved smile, she held a game controller out to Alex. "Take it. The Weird doesn't like to wait."

"Tough," Alex said. "I want to understand more about your past."

Hheilea dropped back to the ground and sat, head bowed, her white hair cascading over her face. Hymeron moved close to her and put an arm around her. "There isn't much to understand. We don't have any home world. Everyone uses or enslaves us. People kill us all the time, and there are fewer and fewer of us left."

Leaning forward, Alex placed a hand on Hheilea's shoulder. "That's terrible. Why are your people treated this way?"

Hymeron's mouth formed a straight angry line across his face. "You think *that's* terrible. Listen to this. It all started when other people in the galaxy found out about us. Our parents' conscious awareness lives in the future. That means they know future possibilities. An adult Kimley risks his health and life whenever he shares that knowledge with another individual. The more it affects the course of the present, the more likely the adult will die if he shares it. It creates chaos in the future possibilities they live in, but others don't care about our lives. A few years ago, one individual killed thousands of Kimleys, trying to learn more about the role of your planet in the future."

"Who?" Alex asked.

Chapter 7

Hheilea jerked her head up to glare at Alex and spat the name. "Maleky."

"Most people are afraid to even say his name," Hymeron said. "Not us, we hate him. He kidnapped one of our cousins."

Alex's face registered his shock and he said, "At least you're safe."

Hheilea gave a short, bitter laugh. She'd never be safe. And soon, her life was going to change forever. She was so frightened. She said, "Our cousin was at the Academy when he was kidnapped, but we're not afraid."

Hymeron nodded. "He was almost as old as my sister, Hheilea, is now. That's the age where we're in the most danger."

"I didn't know you two have a sister," Alex said.

Hheilea shrugged. "It doesn't matter. Someone will probably kidnap her or, if she's lucky, kill her in the attempt. No one cares enough to save m—, her."

Alex reached out to pull both of them into a hug and firmly said, "You said others don't care. Reconsider that statement. I care."

Hheilea held her arms crossed in front of her, as Alex hugged the two of them. It felt so uncomfortable having this boy hold her. She'd never had a friend before, but her reaction to him holding her felt wrong. Why did she start to say to me? He was going to find out she was Hheilea. He was such an idiot. How could he not tell who she was?

"Let's do the video games tomorrow evening," Hymeron said.

Alex said, "Good idea, Hymeron. Do you know the names of those spiral galaxies hanging above us?"

The night sky with stars had reappeared above them. Hheilea found the Weird had her lying in a hammock. Next to her, Alex and Hymeron each lay in separate hammocks suspended from trunks. High above them, feathery fronds moved against the night sky. In the background, she could hear the lapping of waves.

~**********~

Hheilea woke, blinking in the bright morning light. She sniffed the air. Argh, that smell. Every morning— She ground her teeth in frustration. And the Weird wouldn't tell her what was going on. It was like it was teasing her with the flowery fragrance every morning. No use asking the Weird, it wouldn't tell her. She might as well just ignore it. Near her, but on small separate islands surrounded by water, she could see Alex and Hymeron sleeping in their hammocks. She grinned to herself. Alex probably doesn't know the island he was on was really a huge animal. Maybe she could get the Weird to surprise him. That would be fun. Her hammock started to swing. Hheilea grasped the edges of her hammock and spoke to the Weird, |Weird, what are you doing?|

|I'm making your hammock swing| came the smug reply.

Hheilea knew the story about the Weird, how Deems had one adversary whose wisdom had defeated their plans to destroy life in many different solar systems. This had happened again and again until finally, with overwhelming numbers, they were able to capture and kill him. Out of respect and wanting to keep a great foe to practice against, the Deems used a mind copy of the adversary to create the Weird. Hheilea asked the Weird, |Weird, why have you put us into a simulation of my people's home world? You're supposed to be so wise. Didn't you know how painful it would be?|

|Yes, I knew. I'm sorry for your pain.|

Hheilea followed, |Then wh—| Her hammock tipped, almost dumping her out, and Hheilea squealed. |Weird, stop it. You're going to dump me into the sea.|

|No, not the sea. I want you somewhere else.|

In the next instant, Hheilea was lying beside Alex, and he had an arm around her. The music in her head soared, and she rolled out of the hammock. Hheilea backed away quickly, her cheeks burning. She wanted to turn away to hide her embarrassment but couldn't stop staring at Alex. Hheilea's quick exit swung the hammock, and dumped Alex and Hymeron, who had also been deposited into the hammock, onto the sand below. She watched the crazy, entrancing human untangle himself from a struggling Hymeron. Her embarrassment grew at her partial acknowledgement of how she felt about the boy. She repeated to herself. "He's just my friend. He's just my friend."

Alex spit out sand, and asked, "What happened?"

Hheilea said, "For some strange reason the Weird put me in your hammock, and I jumped out."

Alex shrugged. "What? Why did you jump out?" Alex helped

Hymeron to his feet, "Hhy, you're all red. Are you embarrassed? Why—? Oh, well I guess I don't know what's embarrassing for your people."

While Alex rambled, Hheilea went from embarrassed to furious. Why couldn't he tell she was almost a woman? She wanted to slap him and took two angry steps toward him before regaining control and turning her back, saying, "I'm sorry. Being dumped into your hammock startled me."

Alex brushed himself off and awkwardly laughed. "Oh well, no harm done." Changing topics he asked, "Hhy? Something's been bothering me since last night. How come I haven't heard of your sister before?"

Hheilea froze. What could she say? She looked at her brother. They both turned to Alex and spoke at the same time.

Hheilea said, "She isn't on the ship."

Hymeron said, "She stays hidden in our rooms with Mom."

Alex asked, slowly puzzling things out, "Aren't your rooms on this ship?"

Again both Kimleys answered at once.

Hymeron said, "I meant our rooms back at the Academy."

Hheilea said, "We aren't supposed to tell people she's on the ship."

Alex crossed his arms and frowning said, "You two are hiding something."

Again, the two Kimleys looked at each other. Hymeron shrugged and Hheilea turned to Alex. "I'm sorry, but for her safety we don't talk about her."

In a rush and sounding a little desperate, Hymeron said, "Today we teach you how to play videogames, and Alex, you're so going to get beat."

"Ha!" Alex exclaimed. "You should know that videogames are a teenage boy's favorite pastime in my world. You might not beat me as easily as you expect." In a more serious tone, he continued, "It's okay if you don't trust me with information about your sister, but please, don't lie. Everything's so strange. I don't know who to trust."

Hheilea hesitantly came up to Alex and gave him a hug. "I'm sorry, Alex. I do trust you. I—"

Interrupting, Hymeron spoke up louder than normal. "If

Practice

you're good at videogames, the Weird will just make it harder all that much sooner."

Alex pushed Hheilea away forcing her to break the hug. He nervously cleared his throat. "Okay, Hymeron. Let's get started."

Hheilea nodded her head and swallowed as she looked back up at his intense blue eyes. She glanced over at Hymeron's worried expression and backed away from Alex.

~**********~

The next few days, they did exercise activities during the day, followed by videogames in the evening. One evening, Hymeron said, "You're doing great. I'm looking forward to tomorrow. We get to be in the game."

"What do you mean 'in the game'?" Alex asked.

"It'll be easier to show you," Hheilea said.

The next morning, the Kimleys wore shorts and running shoes, with their white hair tied back in ponytails. Hymeron had ditched his shirt and vest, but Hheilea still had on a tight vest. In her hands she held a semi-translucent mass. "This is your new type of controller. It's a computer and much more."

Alex held up a hand and walked up to Hheilea. "Wait. I've wanted to ask why you're so different. Do Kimley boys change as they get older?"

Hheilea's voice squeaked as she answered the question with a question. "What do you mean?"

Hymeron tried to interrupt. "We need to get going."

Alex moved closer to Hheilea. "Your voice is higher than Hymeron's, your legs are very slender compared to his, and your hips are wider. And your face is shaped much differently. Like how I think an elven—."

Hymeron shoved between them. "Come on, we have to explain your new controller. Stop being goofy. Of course everyone's different."

Alex held his hands up in surrender. "Okay. How do I use this?"

Hheilea said, "Kneel in front of me."

When Alex knelt, she laid the mass on his head. His hair started poking through, and she chuckled at how funny he looked. Amazingly fast, the mass sank down through his hair, and his head looked normal again except right at the edges of his hair. She restrained an impulse to smooth his hair. "It's your personal, artificial intelligence or AI for short. Stand-up and look at my scalp. Both Hymeron and I have one too. It interfaces with your brain. With your AI you'll be able to communicate with other people and access other computers. Eventually, it'll develop its own personality." As she spoke, Alex looked down into her eyes. Her heart beat faster and she wanted him to— Troubled by her reaction, Hheilea turned her view to the ground and finished talking. "This AI will always be with you. Physically, I think you're doing great. Now we're going to help you learn things to survive out in the real world."

"Let's get started," Hymeron sighed impatiently. "He'll catch on."

Suddenly, Hheilea stood with Alex and Hymeron on an eight-foot by eight-foot platform of grass. In front of it, other platforms, some short and some long, floated in the air. To the right and to the left, stone walls stretched forward out of sight. Alex moved to the edge of the platform and looked under it. Quickly, he backed up. "This platform is floating."

Hymeron shrugged. "Sort of. It's just like the first videogame we played, except now you're inside the game. The goal is to find the coins and exit to the next level without dying. After you finish this game, we're doing one where we can fight with swords. I'm looking forward to it."

"Without dying?" Alex asked, his voice squeaking. "I thought the Weird wouldn't kill anyone."

"You don't physically die," Hheilea said. "You won't feel pain if you miss a jump or get caught in a trap, like that one." She pointed toward a set of tall, sharp stakes standing in a pit. "You just lose a game life and find yourself on a grass platform like this at the beginning of the level. If you lose too many lives, the game is over and you lose. I hope you beat this game quickly."

She watched the boys. Hymeron jumped to another platform, a wooden one, and Alex followed. A little later, Alex jumped at a moving grass platform, missed it, and let out a yell as he fell. Hheilea resolutely stopped watching Alex fall. Falling really wouldn't hurt him. Beginning herself, she struggled to focus on her own progress.

Practice

Finally, Hheilea, panting from exertion, stood on the last platform. Only then did she give in to her desire to watch. After she waited for a long time, she caught sight of Hymeron. He jumped over a series of spinning rocks and dodged some swinging logs. Alex carefully mimicked Hymeron, following the path he took.

With one last jump the boys joined her on the platform. Immediately, all of them stood on a grassy hill. Above them, fireworks shot off. A victory song started playing.

Alex asked, "Now do we get to use swords?"

"You did a great job using your AI," Hheilea said.

"What?" Alex said. "I didn't need it."

"There's another game we could do. It would force you to use your AI more," Hymeron said with a grin.

Alex frowned. "You said we would do the sword fighting next." He paused and added, "but you said I would be learning things to help me survive in the real world. How will sword fighting help in the real world?"

Hymeron sat down. "The most dangerous threat in the universe is Deems. Their technology is about the best in the universe. Most advanced weapons of your world will have limited use. But Deems love physical fights and swords work great for fighting them. For some Deems, very special swords work the best."

"That's good to know," Alex said. "I remember Ytell talking about Deems and they sound terrible."

Hymeron said, "They are. Did Ytell make clear that they aren't just beasts, but are actually very intelligent, with a higher level of technology than most other civilizations?"

"I think so," Alex said, and then he paused. "It's been a long time since I saw my friends in the flock. I want to get back. How fast can I do this sword training?"

Throughout this discussion, Hheilea didn't say anything. She didn't think they should move on. Alex's comment of not needing to use AI was bad. He needed to spend more time learning to use it. Suddenly it dawned on her - she didn't want Alex to go back to his flock. Being with him was fun. She wanted to stay with him. Confusion, anger, fear, and other emotions she wouldn't put a name to warred within her heart. Hheilea's mouth dropped open at that thought, and adamantly, she shook her head "no" to the thoughts. Hheilea commanded the Weird, |Take us to the sword training.|

The scene shifted, and everything changed. Hheilea stood on top of a stone tower, in the embrasure. A breeze played with her hair and flapped her long, loose, white dress. It took a second for the change to register, and then she became aware of something else. Music, haunting, mesmerizing music, played in her mind. The combination of having her secret identity exposed and acknowledging the music playing ripped a scream from her. "No!"

From below, Hymeron yelled, "Weird! What are you doing?"

Hheilea beat against the stone of the battlement with a fist, and again she screamed, "No!"

She heard Alex and looked down at him and her brother.

In confusion, Alex said, "Where did Hhy go? Who's the pretty woman on the tower?

No one said anything for a long moment, and in a shocked voice Alex answered his own questions. "Hhy and your sister, Hheilea, they're the same person."

Hymeron clutched his hair with both hands. "Yes. I don't know what the Weird's doing. It shouldn't have known about my sister. We've got to get her down. She needs to stay in her disguise."

Hheilea saw an arrow shoot into the ground at Alex's feet, and gave a gasp of fear for him.

Alex jumped back and shouted at Hymeron. "Someone's shooting at me! Why am I hearing music? And why do we need to get her down?"

"Hurry," Hymeron said, sounding desperate. "The Weird's starting this scene."

Another arrow struck near Alex's feet, and he dodged to the side. "Where are these arrows coming from? What am I supposed to do?"

Hymeron said, "The Weird's having the arrows fired at you. Use your AI. Just the same way you used it in the last game. That's how you made those jumps. Get your AI to use the closest gravity generators to lift you. That's the easiest way to go over the wall."

But he didn't use his AI, Hheilea thought. She had to get the Weird to send them back to a practice scene where Alex could learn to use it. But the Weird refused to respond.

Alex ducked behind a stump. "I don't understand. How can

gravity lift me?"

Hymeron spoke quickly. "A gravity generator creates nuclei to pull you or an object toward them. Oh, and Alex, you might want to know you'll feel pain learning to sword fight."

Hheilea watched the scene below while trying to get the scene changed. Below her, Alex collapsed to his hands and knees. Frustrated, angry, and concerned, Hheilea stepped back from the battlement and looked for a trapdoor or some other way down. A scream interrupted her search. She raced back to the embrasure and anxiously scanned the area below. After a moment of searching, she spotted Hymeron gazing up into a tree. She gasped in alarm at seeing Alex's body hanging, jammed between two branches. "Are you okay?"

Alex moved, and she could hear his bitterness as he replied. "Fine, I'm just fine."

Giving up on finding a way down on her own, she continued to watch the events below. Slowly, Alex climbed down from the tree. He moved out into the open and suddenly, he rose straight up into the air, picking up speed as he shot above Hheilea. Up he went, growing smaller and smaller and smaller.... All of a sudden he started to descend, moving faster and faster. "Ahhhhhhh! Stop! Stop me!"

Chapter Eight
Sword Fighting

Hheilea found herself tied to a tree. A short, scruffy man holding a sword stood between her and Alex.

Alex collapsed on the grassy ground. "What happened?"

Hymeron said, "It took us out of that scene before you smashed into the ground and brought you here. You need to get it together."

Hheilea screamed. "Get back up! He's going to hit you with his sword!"

The fighter ran at Alex. "Eeyah!"

At the battle roar, Alex scrambled to his feet. Meanwhile, Hheilea frantically tugged at the ropes. She wanted to avert her eyes, but couldn't. Relief flooded her, as with a clang of steel meeting steel Alex blocked the attack. The next moment she screamed as he stumbled and the enemy's blade sliced toward Alex's throat.

The scene shifted. Hheilea stood in a grassy dell sprinkled with yellow and white flowers with the boys and a tall man.

Alex asked, "What? What just happened?"

A blue and orange butterfly fluttered by Alex toward the tall man wearing a gray robe secured about the waist by a wide leather belt with a jewel-encrusted scabbard. It landed on the black pommel of the man's sword.

"He did a serviceable block," said the stranger, with a harsh voice, "but he needs practice on his footwork. Tripping during an attack is very dangerous. Of course, instead of trying the block, he should've moved in close and gutted his attacker."

"Who are you?" Alex asked.

"I'm Weldon, the legendary sword master," Weldon said, rubbing a scraggly brown beard with one hand as he looked Alex up and down. He turned and looked at Hheilea, giving her an abbreviated bow. "I didn't know we had a young Kimley woman with us. Am I training this boy to help protect you? He isn't going to be proficient for a long time. I could come out and be your knight."

She flushed and opened her mouth to answer, but Hymeron interrupted. "Please keep it a secret. No one's supposed to know about my sister. She's been in disguise as a younger boy. I don't know how or why the Weird took her disguise away." He added to Alex, "Weldon's a computer character."

Again, Weldon stood still, stroking his chin, and absently spoke, looking off into the distance. "Hmmm. I'm going to have a chat with the Weird about this."

Annoyed and frustrated, Hheilea stomped forward, but her long, full dress snagged on a plant. She tugged it free. "Thank you for offering to protect me. I'll think about it."

Weldon said, "That dress isn't very practical for here. If the Weird insists on having you wear it, you could gird your loins."

"What?" she asked, perplexed.

Weldon removed his belt. With a series of movements, he gathered his robe until it was tied a knot in front of his waist. The robe still covered his torso, but from the waist down it looked like a bulky diaper. "I have done this before to get my robe out of the way. Now Alex, pull out your sword, and I'll start your training."

Following Weldon's example, Hheilea gathered the white dress up in front of her thighs, pulled it snug against her backside. A curt command came from Weldon. "Don't watch her."

Hheilea snorted and tucked the excess fabric between her legs and pulled it tight behind her. Gathering half of the material in each hand, she stretched the two ends around her hips and tied them into a knot. Without the dress to bother her, she stomped off into the bushes, and found a tree to sit against. Plopping down on the ground, she tried to ignore the sounds of the sword-fighting practice and her brother shouting words of either encouragement or derision. Closing her eyes, she considered the music she was hearing. Fear and uncertainty tugged at her. It couldn't be the… What else could it be? She stayed there fighting with her own thoughts and ignoring the others' attempts to call her to lunch.

Eventually, the light of day grew dim until the dark shadows in the woods were broken only by the flickering fire in the clearing.

Chapter 8

Weldon and the boys called to her once again. The scent of hot food caused her stomach to growl in complaint of her fast. Alex's voice rose above the rest. "Come on, Hheilea. You have to be getting hungry."

Hymeron said, "When she's mad, it's best just to leave her alone. I'm going to get some more firewood."

Weldon said, "I'll help you."

Hheilea pushed herself up, and knocked the clinging leaves off her legs. She shoved her way through the bushes and stomped into the clearing. Alex stepped quickly toward her. She turned away, but the fire blocked her escape. He touched her shoulder and said, "What's going on?"

She knocked his hand away. "Nothing's going on."

Alex said, "I understand you're upset, but …"

Hheilea shoved at his chest, interrupting him. "You don't understand anything."

She followed up her first shove, intending to push him harder. The firelight lit up his eyes, and for a second, she gazed into them. Notes of music rose and fell, like the crashing of waves, and she shook.

Alex reached out and grasped her arms. "You hear this music too. What does it mean?"

"It doesn't mean anything!" she yelled at him, twisting out of his grasp.

Weldon strode into the clearing and tossed an armful of wood to the ground. He pulled his sword out and pointed to Hheilea. "Take that sword the Weird is offering you and try to hit me."

Hheilea snatched the sword hanging in the air and charged at Weldon, slashing at him from side to side. He backed up, just blocking her blows. They circled the fire, filling the air with the sound of ringing blows. Hymeron charged out of the woods and stopped to stand by Alex. They watched Hheilea slash at the tall man. Finally, Hheilea stopped, dropped her sword, and leaned on her knees, gasping for breath. Weldon slid his sword into its scabbard and untied a leather flask. He offered it to Hheilea. "Here, rinse out your mouth, spit, and take a sip."

Accepting the offer, she poured some of the cool liquid into her mouth, swished it around, and spit into the flames, where it sizzled. Lifting the flask again, she took a sip, swallowed, and then another.

She handed it back to Weldon. "Thanks. I feel better now. Where's the food?"

Putting an arm around her shoulder, Weldon led her to the food.

~**********~

In the weeks following, Hheilea heard Alex try multiple times to talk to Hymeron about the music and ask about the dangers she faced. Each time, Hymeron avoided the questions. She didn't want to talk with Alex about it either, except she had an annoying feeling she should be talking to him instead of just stealing glances at him. She hadn't paid any attention to the music, until the Weird forced her to wear a dress. Alex was just her friend, just her friend…, just her—. The memory of how it felt to be next to him in the hammock warmed her face, she ducked her head down, hoping no one saw her blush.

One warm afternoon, smashing sounds echoed in the woods as Alex defended himself from flying melons with a club. Hheilea leaned up against a tree with her head bowed, hair hanging over her face, and whittled while stealing glances at him. The discarded pieces of wood and occasional gasps of pain from nicking herself with the knife were testaments to how distracting she found him. Peeking at him increased the music which annoyed her, causing her to fiercely attack the piece of wood with her knife. The music would die down. She would sneak a look through her hair at him, only to have the cycle of music start again, along with her anger. Eventually, Hheilea threw down the knife and her latest butchered piece of wood. She stormed off toward the woods, and Hymeron scrambled out of her way.

One step into the woods and the sound of smashing disappeared. Hheilea whirled about. The trees were gone, replaced by an open glade with white flowering bushes and a waterfall. Incensed at the change in scene, she yelled aloud at the Weird, "Oh, and now you'll change the scene for me. I told you Alex needs to go back and do some other games where he can learn easier." She tried again to communicate with the Weird through her AI. |What are you doing? He has to learn how to use his AI.|

She sat in surprise as the Weird answered for the first time since her disguise was taken away. "Hheilea, as a Kimley, you have little reason to trust. But you—"

Hheilea wasn't about to listen to a lecture. She had questions. "Why don't you change the scene to where Alex can be taught to use his AI? Why do you insist on dressing me as a girl? How did you know I'm a girl?"

"Are you going to let me answer or just interrupt?"

She ground her teeth in frustration. "I'll listen."

"As I was starting to say, you need to trust my plans. I—"

Hheilea jumped to her feet and shouted. "What do you mean, your plans? Alex needs to learn how to use his AI."

"Interrupt...or listen?"

She flopped back to the ground and muttered, "Listen."

The Weird continued to speak in her head. "You and Alex have problems, but you need to understand Deems. They're the bigger issue. They created this ship, Weldon, and myself. You should never think of them as just beasts or monsters. They are very intelligent, and their technology in most ways is more advanced than other civilizations. They are the most pompous creatures I know of, and that can trick people into taking them too lightly. However, you can beat them. They aren't the smartest, wisest, or even the best fighters. Weldon was modeled on an amazing fighter who defeated Deems again and again until they used superior forces to capture and kill him. I was modeled on another individual. Whoever it was out-thought Deems a number of times, ruining their plans. I helped the slaves on board this ship overthrow the Deems and capture this ship. Now, I'm working on another way to thwart Deems. I suspect you need to talk you're your father or maybe the Tasties. Alex is important to this plan. You and Hymeron have done well with Alex, but there's much more he needs to learn. He needs to be brought along just right. I know this is a difficult time for you and you're quite emotional, but be patient with me, or you'll distract Alex."

Hheilea's feelings ripped her response out of her mouth. "Emotional? Distract him? He distracts me. It shouldn't be. I shouldn't be attracted to him."

The Weird answered her "Yes, you're distracted by him, and he's distracted by you."

At the second time hearing *he's distracted by you* her heart swelled, the music sounded sweeter, and tremulously she thought to herself. *He loves me*. Adamantly she fought back. He couldn't love her. It would lead to hurt and disappointment for him. She couldn't love him. He was just a boy and a human. Tearing herself from those thoughts she asked, "What are you working on that's so important?"

After a pause, she heard the Weird's answer. "Saving Earth. I need to talk to your dad again. I think you're important for my plans too. Now, be careful with Alex."

The glade disappeared and the sounds of fighting practice echoed through the forest. In a few steps, Hheilea returned to the rest of the group. Alex stood knee-deep in the smashed remains of dozens of melons.

Weldon sat on a branch above everyone, and dropped one last melon at Alex. "That's enough strength training for today. Now we'll work with swords, but with something new added in. I'm happy with your progress. You're starting to anticipate my attacks. That's very important for any form of fighting. Remember to always watch your opponent's eyes. This will help you prepare for their attack. I haven't figured out why your ability to anticipate an attack is worse at times. For example, you weren't doing very good anticipating melons during the last twenty minutes, but the last few times you did great. Also, you need to be quicker with the tierce block. We'll work on it today. I don't know what your schedule is like, but when you have time make sure you come back. Have your AI bring up Weldon, the Sword Master. In a year, I might be willing to admit I taught you."

"Okay," Alex gasped as he smashed the last melons flying at him from all directions. Covered in melon gore he added, "Can I wipe my face off?"

"Better than wipe it off," Weldon gruffly said. "Just get rid of it, like this."

All of the melon gore disappeared from Alex. Where he had just been wading in gore he now stood balanced on a log.

"You could've done the same with your AI. It can communicate with the Weird." Weldon levitated into the sky. "Follow me."

Alex stood on the ground, looking up at Weldon. "I can't get up there."

"What?" Weldon shouted. His face turned a dark red, and his

eyeballs bulged from their sockets. Swooping out of the sky, he shook a fist in Hymeron's face. "You've brought me a wet-behind-the-ears kid who can't even use his AI! This is ridiculous. Come back when he's ready." Weldon exclaimed before vanishing.

Alex threw his club down. "Doesn't he know the Weird is in control of my training? It isn't our fault."

"He'll get over it," Hymeron said.

Hheilea watched the boys in silence. Had she seen Weldon wink at her? The Weird had told her, he had a plan for Alex and it entailed bringing him along just right.

Alex glanced at Hheilea and turned away. "Is Weldon really just a computer character? He has such strong emotions. It's like he's real."

Hheilea didn't try to hide her exasperation. "Of course he's real. Don't you pay attention? Remember him eating fish with us around the fire?"

Alex held his hands up in puzzlement. "What? Either he's a computer character or real."

Remembering the Weird's request to be careful with Alex, Hheilea forced herself to speak in a calmer voice. "Look, he's just another type of AI. Some people call them RE because they have a real existence. You need to talk more to your AI. It won't respond much at first, but it will react to simple requests such as, 'Find a local gravity generator and lift me.' You just need to learn how to define what you mean by 'lift me.' Your AI is learning too. It's essentially a baby, and working with it can be interesting."

Hheilea remembered Alex's first attempts to use his AI and laughed before she continued. "Over time it will learn your ways and, as a result, respond to you better. Also, it grows in ability to fit who you are. I've heard of a few people who manage to develop incredible AI, but we haven't seen anyone do that."

Hymeron stood up. "You're going to play a new game. It's similar to the first game. But first we will eat, and you need some rest."

**Chapter Nine
The First Fight**

In the new game, Hheilea stood on a grassy platform next to a pile of snow. Leaning down, she scooped up some snow and began to make a snowball. The stupid Weird had put her back into pants. She thought briefly of the dress hanging in her closet. It would be fun to wear a dress like it. She grinned, looked at Alex, and turned away. If only the music would stop, she could have fun. She did like Alex, but he was a human and just a boy. Around the three of them floated other platforms, moving in all directions. Scattered about the platforms were tubs of mud, buckets of water, and piles of snow. Hymeron and Alex stood on their own platforms. Green holograms with the number zero floated over both of their heads.

Hymeron tossed a snowball from hand to hand. He threw it, hitting Alex.

"Hey," Alex said.

"Look up," Hheilea said, pointing over Alex's head.

Above Alex flashed a slightly yellow, green hologram with the number one displayed.

"When that number reaches sixty, you lose. Dunking you in a tub of mud is thirty points," Hymeron said. "The color also changes from green to orange as you get hit. Good luck." Then both Kimleys started belting Alex with snowballs.

He jumped toward another platform but missed and plummeted toward the ground. Hheilea stopped throwing snowballs and silently cheered Alex on. Come on Alex, you can do it. Get your AI to move you. Just before Alex hit the ground, his body jerked up into the air. Hheilea grinned at the sight of Alex's success. He flew through the air and tried to land on a different platform, but he had too much forward momentum and tumbled off the far side of it. Hheilea picked up more snow and paused to watch Alex land face first on a lower grass platform.

Hymeron continued to fire snowballs as Alex's hologram turned orange with the numbers rapidly increasing. He asked Hheilea, "What's with you? Keep throwing."

~*********~

Two weeks later, Alex jumped toward a platform. Hheilea fired snowballs at him, but his grass platform flipped up just in time. "Hah—I blocked you this time" Alex replied.

"Look up," Hheilea said, laughing as she used her AI to dump snow onto Alex.

That evening, Hheilea and Hymeron sat beside Alex, holding sticks and roasting a marshmallow-type treat over a lava flow. A barren mountain rose into an orange sky. Out of the mountain top, a fountain of lava shot a thousand feet into the air. The crescent of a giant planet hung above them, filling most of the sky. Hheilea watched her treat slowly browning and said to Alex, "You're quiet tonight. Are you getting discouraged?"

"I just want to be done and get back to the flock. We've been in the Weird's world forever. I'm still puzzled about how it makes these worlds, and I really don't understand what the Weird is. You've said it's a computer, but other times, it sounds like another AI."

Hheilea didn't like Alex's desire to be back with his flock, but she tried to be logical. It would be good for him to get away from her. She didn't want him to get hurt, and she'd tell her dad that something was wrong with her t'wasn't-to-be-is. Except, had she heard of a t'wasn't-to-be-is ever being wrong about who it brought together? A bubble in the lava popped, throwing tendrils of lava up into the air. Hheilea jerked her treat back. One of the tendrils hit Hymeron's marshmallow treat, melting into it, and in a second, flames covered the remains of the treat.

Hymeron tossed the stick onto the lava where it burst into flames. He held a hand out, and another stick with a marshmallow treat appeared. With a long sigh, Hymeron looked at Alex. "The Weird is another AI, and it's in a computer of its own. You're supposed to figure your AI out on your own. I've enjoyed the break from all of my plans and ventures, but you're taking forever. Your

AI interfaces with other computers."

Alex said, "I'm trying, but you're making it too hard."

"I'm sorry. Don't give up. You're getting better," Hheilea said.

Hymeron poked his sister. "Stop being such a softy. He's pretending. Trying to get us to take it easier and give him a chance to beat us."

Hheilea looked at Alex just in time to catch him grinning, before he hid it with a pretend yawn. She gazed at him in surprise, and he shrugged and winked at her. He had made a fool of her on purpose. Hheilea jumped to her feet and tossed her stick down. "Come on, Hymeron, let's go to our room and get some sleep."

"Okay. I'm coming. Just don't act so bossy." Hymeron pulled his sticky treat off the stick he held and popped it into his mouth.

The next day, Hheilea stood next to Hymeron on a platform. Again, they encouraged Alex to gain a better understanding of how to use his AI, even as they worked at beating him. Hheilea shouted at Alex, "You're moving much better through the air. I think you've made a breakthrough with your AI. Did you practice last night?"

Alex didn't answer, and she lost sight of him. "Where did Alex go?"

Hymeron shouted, "He's over here."

She saw Hymeron throwing snowballs at Alex, but he suddenly stopped and threw his hands up. "He's just standing there. What's he trying to do? We're going to be stuck in here forever."

Hheilea joined him. "No, Alex is up to something."

Hymeron said, "Are you—."

Alex disappeared. Hheilea gasped and looked around trying to spot him. "Where did he go?" Balls of sloppy mud started pummeling her.

"Over here!" Hymeron shouted, jumping onto a platform to escape the blizzard of mud. Hheilea jumped after him. Something shoved her, and she crashed into Hymeron.

"Aaahh! You're knocking me off!" Hymeron slid toward the edge.

"No, the platform's tipping us off!" With a splash she landed in cold, soupy mud with her brother.

"I hope I wasn't too rough on you little kids," Alex exclaimed from above them.

Covered in mud, Hheilea stood with her fists on her hips. "I'm

Chapter 9

not a little kid." She laughed. "You did it."

Hymeron also said, "I'm not a little kid either."

Alex didn't look at Hymeron. He only had eyes for Hheilea. The human boy stood looking back at her. His triumphant look faded, his face turned red, and he mumbled. "No, you're definitely not a little kid." Jumping off his platform, he flipped through the air. "I'm finally starting to enjoy this. You know, I've really gotten to like you two. This training has been fun, and I'm feeling much stronger. But I'd like to return to my flock."

"You're not done yet," Hymeron said. "The Weird says you need to go back to the castle and rescue the fair maiden." He grumbled discontentedly. "At least no RE that can leave the computer world has seen that Hhy is actually Hheilea, except for Weldon. And he is the epitome of trustworthiness."

~**********~

Hheilea found herself back on the stone tower in a dress. Resignedly she looked down at it, but then smiled. It was like the dress in her closet. She pirouetted and sighed to herself. If only there was a young Kimley man with her. Frowning, she walked over to the crenelated, stone edge of the tower. Peering over the edge, she called out. "Alex, save me and we can get out of here."

Below, she saw Alex smoothly rise up from the ground into the air. Hheilea gasped at the sight of archers preparing to shoot Alex. She took a breath to scream a warning, but before she could, the archers were all wrapped up in ropes. Relaxing, she grinned in relief. He was doing great. They'd be out of the Weird soon. Alex continued through the air toward her and then slammed to a stop. She almost laughed aloud at the sight of his face smashed against an invisible wall, but a guttural cry from below drew her eyes down. At first she couldn't see anything, but the voice sent a chill down her spine.

"Are you ready to challenge me?"

"What are you?" Alex asked, looking down toward the base of the tower.

Fighting a queasy feeling, Hheilea leaned forward to look down at the other speaker. Alex was going to be okay. They'd be out of there soon. A huge, black figure stood in front of the door to the tower. Two big, scaly wings flapped from the figure's back. Even from this distance, Hheilea could see its blazing red eyes. Hheilea's eyes went wide, and she stifled a scream.

The black figure's whip-like tail lashed behind it. A big, toothy grin creased the figure's face. "I'm a Gaahr, one of the Deem. We are the most powerful creatures of the universe. My name is Gagugugul. You are doomed."

Alex laughed at the pompous statement.

The Gaahr stood dressed in only dark-red and gold leather straps. Some areas of its body were blurred by something Hheilea couldn't see. A necklace hung from his neck. He was twice the size of Alex!

Ropes appeared around the monster, and disappeared just as quickly. "You can't defeat me with that kind of trick. I work with the Weird." With a clawed hand, Gagugugul drew a huge sword from a scabbard. "I hope Weldon taught you how to fight with a sword, little boy. I want to have fun defeating you."

Placing a hand on the pommel of his sword, Alex drifted slowly downward. The Gaahr stretched out his thirty-foot wings and rose to meet him. Alex paused, and Hheilea could hear the uncertainty in his voice as he faced this terror. "I think I'll call you Gargle. How do you know Weldon?"

"We fight together sometimes," Gargle said. "I like him."

Hheilea responded, her voice full of concern, "Alex, be careful. You can't trust Deems."

Alex glanced up at her then away.

Gargle laughed. "A young Kimley woman and she has a problem."

"What do you mean?" Alex demanded, moving closer to the Deem.

"The Weird knows even if you don't," Gargle said. Lifting his head, he hollered at Hheilea, "A green crystal will help you!"

Alex said, "I thought Deems were terrible creatures. You look fearsome but sound quite reasonable."

"Well you see, for now, I'm a tame Deem locked inside the computers," Gargle said.

"Then step aside," Alex said, "and I won't have to hurt you."

Gargle laughed. "You insult me by your offer. In this crazy world of the Weird, will fire still burn you?" Then he roared, "I am

Chapter 9

a Deem! I look forward to tasting your flesh."

Alex drifted backwards. "I'm not afraid of you. You sound like a buffoon."

"Then prove it," Gargle said. "Pull your little toothpick out and let's start this dance." He opened his mouth wide and laughed a tremendous bellow of a laugh.

The Weird shouldn't have Alex fighting a Deem. He could get seriously hurt. Hheilea tried to communicate with the Weird, but it ignored her.

Below, Alex paused. Squaring his shoulders, he slid his sword out of its scabbard.

Gargle roared and fell back. "The Weird is cheating! It gave you a string-sword."

Hheilea grinned. Now he should be okay…if he just remembers his training.

"Who are you?" Alex said in a puzzled tone, but he wasn't looking at Gargle.

Hheilea edged farther out over the edge, trying to see who Alex was talking to.

Alex almost dropped his sword and said out loud in evident confusion, "What's going on?" He tentatively moved into the guard position. His right arm was slightly bent with the sword tip pointed at empty air. The sword glowed along the cutting edge, leaving behind a trail of light as it cut through the air. Alex slashed and stabbed at the air in front of him.

Stunned by his behavior, Hheilea leaned dangerously out from the stone. At the last minute, she pressed her hands against the stone to stop from falling. "What are you doing?"

"What?" Alex stopped to look toward her.

"Look out!" Hheilea and Hymeron shouted at the same time.

Gargle attacked from below, slashing at Alex's legs.

Alex spun in the air, his feet flipping up over his head. He slashed down with his sword. Light trailed in an arc as the blade descended at the rising Gargle.

Wings beating frantically, Gargle tried to switch course. Now his blade rose in a block against Alex's attack. A ringing "snap" sounded the moment the edge of Alex's sword sliced into and broke off the Deem's sword. Gargle threw away the useless stub.

"But he warned me," Alex said. He hung in the air, slowly

rotating back to right-side-up.

Gargle circled to Alex's back. Hheilea gasped and tried to shout another warning, but fear for Alex froze her. Why wasn't he attacking the Deem?

Alex shifted his grip to clench his sword, and moved away from Gargle.

Hymeron yelled, "What are you doing? Gargle's in the other direction!"

Alex swung his sword like a club, bashing at something. The blows stopped as if something in the air blocked them.

"He's fighting someone," Gargle said and laughed, adding, "I think someone's in his mind."

Suddenly, Alex changed direction to charge at Gargle. His sword beat down at the fearsome, black creature.

"You're going to lose. It's been foreseen," Gargle gasped out as he tried to defend himself. The light-trailing sword bit into his body. Smoke rose each time Alex hit him, accompanied by a sizzling sound similar to a welder cutting through thick metal. Hheilea gasped and her eyes widened at the battle below. One of Gargle's clawed hands ripped Alex's side. Forgetting her location, Hheilea leaned too far forward and lost her balance. She opened her mouth to scream.

~**********~

Hymeron, Alex, and Hheilea stood in the empty Weird room surrounded by white walls. She choked off her scream. A holo-field formed around Alex's torso and one arm as he slumped toward the ground. Hheilea recovered from her brief moment of disorientation to catch him. She slipped an arm around him so he could lean on her.

"Can we ... get ... out of here?" Alex asked, panting. He coughed and threw up all over Hheilea.

Hymeron backed away from them. "You two need to get cleaned up. We can't leave until the holo-field heals your wounds. The Weird doesn't want to get in trouble for letting you leave wounded. In fact, you should see Gursha or there'll be a scars. What were you doing back there?"

"I, uh ..." Alex paused and said with more confidence, "I fought

Chapter 9

Gargle and killed him after his claws tore into me ... There was someone or something else."

As he spoke, the splattered liquid disappeared leaving only a faint smell of vomit.

Hheilea said, "After you drew your sword, you asked, 'What's going on?' And you fought something we couldn't see. You weren't fighting Gargle. After Gargle attacked you from below and you fought him off, you stopped and confessed that you had been warned."

Alex shook his head. "My memory of the fight's confusing. It's like something was there, but I can't remember clearly. I drew my sword and... Gargle attacked me from below. I fought him off and ... charged him. I guess I attacked kind of foolishly. Weldon would've been upset with me."

"What do you mean 'would've?'" Hymeron asked. "He is upset."

"What?" Alex asked. "He wasn't there."

"He's an RE. Of course he was watching," Hymeron said. "He and Gargle are probably talking about the fight right now."

Hheilea grasped Alex's arm. "We better get going. We're supposed to take you to Amable's office after we're done. Don't forget, my name is Hhy and I'm a boy. Never refer to me as Hheilea or as a girl."

Alex looked back at her. "Yes, Hheilea -- I mean *Hhy*."

Hheilea shook her head at him. "You're hopeless. Try not to do anything stupid."

She started to take a step, but the music temporarily overwhelmed her sense of balance, and she tripped, pulling on Alex. He braced himself and kept her from falling. Breathlessly, she looked up into Alex's blue eyes.

Alex grinned at her. "I'll try not to do anything clumsy either."

Hymeron tugged and yelled at both of them. "Come on! Stop your foolishness!"

Hheilea avoided looking at Alex, as they left the Weird. She considered the months they had spent together there. The human teenager beside her was tanned, obviously much stronger, and walked with an assurance born of his experiences. Alex had really worked hard, and the last few days he made amazing progress with his AI. Ahead of her, Hymeron stopped and knocked at Amable's office. Hheilea looked around in surprise.

The door opened, and Amable said, "Come in. Come in."

The three of them stepped through the doorway, and Stick's voice, rising in near panic, greeted Hheilea. "What happened to you? Your shirt's all torn and bloody."

At first, she looked down at her vest in confusion, until she heard Alex speaking from beside her.

"Sorry. I didn't realize how bad it looks. The Gaahr injured me at the end of my training."

Amable crowded past Hheilea to snatch Alex's hand and pumped it up and down. "Congratulations on facing a Gaahr."

"You should've seen him," Hheilea said proudly. "He finished everything Gursha wanted him to do, and the link he's developed with his AI is already better than what I can do. The AI itself is changing and growing to meet his demands."

Amable beamed. "Of course Alex did great. He's quite the boy."

Alex stood still for a second. "Uh, yeah. I really wasn't that great." Changing the topic, he asked, "What's the rest of the flock doing now?"

"Today was their third day in the Hall of Flight," Amable answered.

"But," Alex said. "Their first day was months ago."

Amable laughed. "You've a lot to learn, Alex. Only three days have passed for us. You and the Kimley kids have been in a time bubble."

"A time ..." Alex began and instead asked, "What should I do now?"

"Your clothes are a great badge of courage, but get them changed and have a late lunch with the Kimleys. Afterwards, come back here," Amable said.

Hheilea let the boys lead the way to lunch. She remained quiet, absorbed in her own thoughts. The music wasn't stopping. She shouldn't be hearing it around Alex. He was a crazy human and only a boy. How could he, an alien, be the one chosen for her? One thing she remembered and knew without a doubt, the t'wasn't-to-be-is never was wrong. She knew Hymeron wouldn't be willing to accept any of this. He'd even talked to her about doing something to prevent her t'wasn't-to-be-is from happening. What was going to happen?

Chapter Ten
T'wasn't-to-be-is

Hheilea walked down the corridor on the way back from lunch. She kept looking at Alex. He should've listened to her.

Hymeron snickered and said, "Hheilea told you the spicy, lillyputi dessert can be addictive."

Sweat ran down Alex's face. "I can't forget it. I need more." He stopped to sniff the air. Grasping his shirt, he jerked it to his mouth, and sucked on a spot where the dessert had spilled, and sighed with pleasure.

Hheilea took Alex's arm and began urging him on toward Amable's office. At first, Alex let her, but after a couple of steps, he slowed and looked back the way they had come.

She tugged at Alex's arm but couldn't get him to move. "I need your help, Hymeron. If we can get him to Amable's office, he can use *state of mind* to remove the addictive effects."

Alex leaned away from them. "Come on. Let me go back for seconds."

Hymeron tugged on Alex's hand. "I think that dessert will need to be placed on the restricted list for humans."

"Amable's office is just a few feet farther," Hheilea said, struggling to keep Alex moving the right way.

Hymeron kicked at the door, causing it to slide open.

Hheilea hung from Alex's hand, her feet dragging, as Alex walked back the way they had come. "Amable, we need some help."

"I'm coming," Amable said.

Alex dragged her and Hymeron back down the passageway.

From behind them came Amable's voice. "What's going on?"

"Alex ate some lillyputi dessert," Hheilea said. "He's trying to go back."

Alex said, "I've got to have more."

Amable said, "It's my favorite dessert too."

Still getting dragged backward, Hheilea snapped, "Amable!"

Amable said, "Yes. Just relax, Alex. We all love you. Everything's going to be fine."

Alex slowly stopped dragging the Kimleys. He glanced down at them with a confused expression. "What just happened?"

"You had an addictive reaction to a dessert," Hymeron said. "Amable helped by calming you."

Alex looked even more confused.

Amable gestured toward his office. "Come into my office, and I'll explain."

Approaching the office, Alex began to hear a song playing. "Where's the music coming from?"

Once in the office, Amable pointed to a plant occupying one corner of the room. Its leaves were large and translucent, filled with liquid and with fish-like creatures swimming in them.

Hheilea stopped. More music she didn't want to hear. "Is it just starting to play the ode? I don't want to be here for it."

Amable brushed some dust off his clothes. "The *Ode of Remembrance* finished playing a little while ago. Now, about what I did, you'll learn one of the effects from exposure to Dark Matter can be the ability to change the state of another creature's mind. The more you care for them the better it works. I can encourage others around me to be at peace. I did that for your mind."

Hheilea watched Alex who gazed with wide eyes at Amable.

In response, Amable waggled his bushy eyebrows and chuckled. "I suppose you're wondering if I can hypnotize you. The answer is no. There's a more enslaving way of affecting someone else's mind. You'll learn about it in the Controlling Animals class."

Amable looked at each of them. "Alex, earlier the boys gave me a glowing report of your training. Is there anything you would like to add? Did anything … out of the ordinary happen?"

Alex's mouth opened and shut before he said, "When I drew the sword to fight the Gaahr, Hymeron and Hhei— say I started acting strange and fought something they couldn't see."

"Can you remember—?" Amable gave a sigh and opened a drawer in his desk. "Gursha wants to see you this evening. Work with her to figure out this mystery and give me a call if you need help. For now, take the afternoon off. The boys can show you around. Your flock leader, Ytell, will be in touch with you sometime today."

"How will I call you? I don't think my cell phone works here." Alex said.

Amable paused his rummaging in the drawer to look at Alex and laugh. "Cell phone? Oh, that's a good joke. Contact me through your AI. If you want to talk to me, just think, 'I need to talk to Amable.' Most of us have some form of AI. Stick's AI is how he interfaces with the files and the paperwork he's always working with. Everyone from Earth is receiving their own AI." Amable pulled a disc from the drawer. "Good, here it is. Hymeron, take this with you just in case Alex has a relapse of his addiction. Just aim the pointy end at him and push this button. He'll lose consciousness for a little while. It isn't dangerous, but make sure you don't play with it. Please, bring it back tomorrow."

Hymeron took the small disc. "Great, this will be fun. See ya."

Hheilea said, "Is it a good idea to give him a stunner?" She could imagine Hymeron running through the corridors stunning everyone.

Amable grinned in response. "Have you heard the saying, 'Give a man enough rope and he'll hang himself?' Consider this another test for you and your brother. If I hear any reports of people falling unconscious, I'll know who to blame and will have no qualms about restricting the two of you to your quarters. Besides, Alex really might have a relapse in the next few hours."

Hheilea scowled. "I wouldn't trust Hymeron with it. You should've given it to me. It's going to be your fault if something goes wrong. Come on, Alex, let's go."

"I'll be with you in a second," Alex said. "Amable?"

"Yes, my boy?"

"Did you know something strange is going on with me?"

Hhcilca hcard the beginning of the conversation as she left. Concern for Alex slowed her footsteps, but she resolutely continued on. She wanted to respect his privacy. Hymeron stopped to listen, and she whispered, "Come on," and gave him her big sister glare.

Hymeron shrugged and continued with her. After a while, they heard Alex jogging after them. "Sorry I took so long. Let's go see my flock."

"You just want to see A'idah," Hymeron said with a grin as they waited for Alex.

"What?" Alex asked with an innocent expression, as he caught up.

Hymeron elbowed him. "I saw you look all googly-eyed at her in the clinic."

Hheilea bit her lip at the conversation. *He's mine.* After the t'wasn't-to-be-is no one ever thinks romantically of another but their partner. She gasped at her own thought.

Alex said, "No, not me. Well, maybe some at first. You know it's been very confusing for me. Okay, that was lame. You know she's much younger than me. I think she's only twelve, and I'm fifteen. What about you? How old are you?"

"I'm ten," Hymeron said and added, emphasizing the first three words, "and my brother is eleven. In the next five years, I'll make all the decisions for my adult life."

Hheilea scowled, looking down at her feet. She didn't like this lying to Alex. She was actually about the same age as Alex, except she'd be an adult after her t'wasn't-to-be-is. What would it do to him? Would he grow up and start acting like an adult?

Alex looked at Hymeron. "Really? You guys don't seem that young. Why would you make those decisions so young?"

Hheilea spoke quickly before she could change her mind. "When we turn fifteen, we eventually start hearing a song. It's the beginning of our becoming adults. We're adults and almost always married before we are sixteen." Bitterly she added, "Then we lose touch with *now*."

"But why am I hearing—." Alex started to ask, and then he said, "No way. I'd be getting married soon, and I'm way too young for that. What do you mean *losing touch with now?*"

Hymeron said, "You need to meet our family. I'm warning you, for most people it's a crazy experience."

Hheilea walked along with them, stealing looks at Alex. Occasionally, she caught him looking at her. Neither one said anything. The song, crashing of waves on a distant shore and tinkling of wind chimes, mesmerized her, until she walked into a corner of the corridor. She tried to regain control. It helped when she saw Alex doing the same thing. He looked away from her, and Hheilea laughed to herself, breathing deep. She'd been frightened of this transition to being an adult. She had been troubled by how young Alex was, but as crazy as he was she really did love him. The confusion was still there, but something else, a feeling of rightness, began to grow. Yet, he was so immature. She'd have to help him. The t'wasn't-to-be-is was always right.

They stopped at the door to her home. A red haze settled over them, and a voice asked, "Are you intending or planning any harm to this family?"

"No," both Kimleys said, and then they looked at Alex.

"No. I'm not," Alex said, truthfully.

The voice said as the door slid open, "You are cleared to enter, but an anomalous reading for Alex is noted in the records."

Stepping into the room, Hheilea looked around. For the first time she felt self-conscious about her home. How did Alex see all of this? The colors of the walls changed as she looked at them. The colors flowed from one wall to another. A stack of different-sized bowls rested on the top of a green three-foot tall column. Several other columns with stacks of things, a table on the other side and four chairs, filled the room. Hheilea looked at everything and then at Alex.

He gazed open-mouthed at everything. Her dad, his multicolored hair shimmering like butterfly wings, walked out of a passageway. He didn't look at them. Instead, he looked back the way he came, yelling, "Hymeron, leave your sister alone!" Almost covered by shoulder-length hair, a green lizard stood on his shoulder, looking at them with jewel-like eyes. The man turned back toward the doorway and shouted, "Don't do that!"

"Alex, meet my dad. Dad, this is Alex," Hymeron said.

"He was happy to meet you," the lizard on the man's shoulder said.

Alex held his hand out in greeting, but the man didn't respond. "Why is he yelling at you two and you're not even where he's yelling?"

"He's responding to some future, maybe not even one that will come to pass. Lately, Dad has been worse than normal. It's like he overdosed on lillyputi dessert."

The man hurried to the bowls and grabbed one out of the middle of the stack, leaving the bowls above it hovering in the air. The hovering bowls slowly settled down onto those below. Meanwhile, the man walked across the room and held the bowl at the edge of the table. The only thing on the table was a pedestal, with a pile of beads on it. After a moment, he put the bowl back. The stack of bowls adjusted itself to accept the bowl back into the stack.

"Over there's my mom," Hymeron said, pointing past a cluster of columns with their stacks.

Alex raised his hand in greeting to the woman, but she just sat still, not looking at him. Hymeron walked into the room and slipped the bottom bowl off the column.

"Why's she just sitting?" Alex asked Hheilea. "And what's up with the lizards?"

Hheilea turned a sad expression to Alex. "Mom shared too much of what she sees in the future. That made her view of the future so chaotic, she almost went catatonic. She's getting better."

"The lizards are Cadleys. We all have them. When we're young, they come and go, but after our fourteenth birthday, they stay with us most of the time. It's a symbiotic relationship. We provide a safe place with food, and they help us with living in the now."

Hheilea moved her hair out of the way, and a bright green Cadley scampered out of Hheilea's white hair. "Here, meet Neet. When I'm out in public, Neet has to stay hidden. We don't want anyone to know how old I am."

Neet tipped her head back and forth looking at Alex. "Hold your hand out," Hheilea requested.

On the other side of the room, Hymeron set the bowl on a chair below the edge of the table, sat down and rested his head on the table.

Alex held his hand out, and Neet jumped onto it and scampered up to his shoulder.

Hheilea heard Neet's question in her mind. *Can I taste his ear wax?*

Alex's eyes snapped wide open.

Hheilea said, "What?"

"I heard something in my mind. A voice whispered to me," Alex said.

Hheilea's expression changed to one of wonder and amazement. "You shouldn't have heard that. No one but a Kimley can hear Cadleys' telepathy, and their thoughts are heard by only a Cadley's symbiotic partner or the mate of its partner. Neet asked

Chapter 10

me if she could taste your earwax. It's a delicacy for them."

The tinkling of wind chimes rising and falling like waves on a shore rose to a roar in her mind. Distracted by the music, she almost didn't hear Alex's answer, but she did notice how his eyes got wide when the music roared.

"Yeah, sure. The music, why's it so loud?" And then Alex grinned. "She's tickling me."

Hheilea took Neet back. She had to go get dressed for the t'wasn't-to-be-is. Her time had come. All of her confusion and doubts disappeared. She looked intently at Alex and spoke firmly. "This is our time. Wait for me."

Quickly, she ran to her room. Eagerly, she tore off her clothes and pulled a beautiful white dress from her closet. With fluid movements, she slipped it on. Leaving her room, she spotted the t'wasn't-to-be plant. The strange plant grew in an oval glass pot filled with water. At the base of the pot was the seed the plant grew from. The seed dangled from a flower of the same plant that grew from the seed. As she looked, flesh of a fruit rapidly started covering the seed.

Alex stood gazing at the plant too, and he said in a dream-like voice, "What's that?"

A panicked Hymeron yelled at Alex, "Get out of here!"

Hheilea hurried out of the passageway and brushed past Hymeron. She could see the confusion in his face. Hheilea wished her little brother wasn't so confused about Alex and herself. Her t'wasn't-to-be-is ceremony was going to be wonderful.

Mesmerized by the music, Hheilea stepped to the beat that rhythmically pulled her toward Alex. Her gaze locked on his blue eyes. She felt herself drowning in them as she stepped toward him. She reached for him. Their hands touched, and the world around her disappeared.

Chapter Eleven
Control

Blinking, Alex struggled to sit up, but vertigo threatened his consciousness, and he laid back down. Light brown walls surrounded him and Hymeron. "What happened?"

Hymeron stood, back to the door, glaring at Alex. He pointed down at Alex. "You idiot. You began to dance the t'wasn't-to-be-is dance with my sister. What do you remember?"

Irritation at Hymeron's words and aggressive tone cleared the fog in Alex's mind. "A figure coming toward me. It was Hheilea. She was so beautiful. And then ... I don't remember any more. Where is she? What happened?"

"She's in her room. She's an idiot too. What were you thinking? You shouldn't be dancing the t'wasn't-to-be-is dance with her."

"Get out of my face, Hymeron. Back off. I didn't dance it on purpose."

"Maybe you didn't you—, but the result's the same. I stopped the t'wasn't-to-be-is from finishing. She's my sister, and I'm not about to share her with you. Plus, you're an alien and it isn't right for you to be one with her."

Alex struggled to get up. How did the little kid stop the... What was it? T'wasn't-to-be-is? One with her? "You what?!" He'd been abducted, once by the aliens. But this... t'wasn't-to-be-is... wasn't it abducting him again?

"I used the device Amable gave me." Hymeron stepped closer, getting in the way of Alex getting up. "I knocked both of you out. I carried Hheilea back to her room, and I dragged you to this storage room. I was lucky no one saw me in the passageway."

Alex shoved against the boy's legs. Hymeron had abducted him! Furious, he wanted to beat him up. But the thought that Hymeron was really just a kid stopped him; yet, the fool had stolen

Chapter 11

something from him. The music and Hheilea were both wonderful. "I tried to get you and Hheilea to explain about the music I was hearing during the last months, but you wouldn't. You kept ignoring me, saying I was imagining things. I knew Hheilea was hearing it too. How did it force me into the dance with Hheilea? What is this dance?" Other questions he didn't want to ask Hymeron filled his mind. Where was Hheilea? He wanted to be with her. What was happening to him?

"The dance marks the beginning of two Kimleys' transition to adulthood. We say the music is their future calling to them and bringing them together. Those who dance together ... I don't know why or how you're caught up in this. It's wrong! You can't dance the t'wasn't-to-be-is."

Alex winced at the forcefulness of Hymeron's voice. He struggled to both understand what the boy said and to be reasonable even though he wanted to just scream. "What does t'wasn't-to-be-is mean?"

Hymeron leaned over Alex still glaring and breathing hard. He closed his eyes and began speaking as if from rote. "T'wasn't-to-be-is speaks of the adult life the Kimley participants are moving into and uses a mix of tenses we are familiar with. Adults can move through and experience multiple possible futures. They experience the future in their present tense, but the thing is they can experience futures that probably can't happen. Those futures are called by my people, 'it-was-not-to-be' or 'twasn't-to-be'. Sometimes, the twasn't-to-be future ends up happening and therefore is. That future has become a *t'wasn't-to-be-is*. There's a legend among my people. It says our whole species is working to make a future a long time away, which is extremely unlikely, happen. It is called the '*t'wasn't-to-be-is* legend.' The term also refers to what you started to experience, and I hate all of it. My sister isn't going to do it!"

"Thanks. I understand better," Alex said. How could they live in the future? What was Hymeron's problem? What was it like?

"You don't understand anything. Becoming an adult for a Kimley is terrible. I'm not going to do it, and I don't want to lose my sister to it either

As Alex opened his mouth to ask another question, Hymeron said "We need to get you back to your flock. Don't tell others about this and don't go looking for Hheilea."

Alex began to stand up when Hymeron pushed against his shoulder, shoving him down.

"Stop," Hymeron said.

Alex froze, clenching his hands, and growled, "Now what's wrong?" He was going to beat…

Hymeron started rubbing at Alex's hair. Instead of angry, now his voice was frantic. "It won't come off."

"Stop that! What won't come off?"

Sitting back with a stunned expression, Hymeron looked into Alex's eyes, and then he tipped his head to the side. "See the iridescent scales on the skin of my temples?"

"Yeah. What about them?"

"When I start to become an adult, those scales move from my temples into my hair. I'll end up looking like my dad with iridescent colors shimmering as my hair moves."

At first Alex didn't understand, but in the next moment his mouth dropped open, and he frantically looked about the room, hoping to find something he could see his hair in.

"It shouldn't be, but it is" Hymeron said. "The hair on your temples is starting to get the fine scales that'll give your hair similar color to my dad's hair."

"No! Oh, no. I'm going to look like your dad?"

"My dad looks good."

Alex took a deep breath. He could really use Amable and his ability to calm others. This was just too strange. He was just a teenager and a human. He was not an alien.

Hymeron continued speaking, "You have to stay here. I'm going to figure out a plan to deal with you."

"No!" Alex shot to his feet and, with his superior strength and size, shoved Hymeron against the wall. "You are not going to make any plans for me. I've had it with everyone and everything controlling me. I'm going to take care of this."

Hymeron stared back and Alex looked down to see Hymeron pulling the stunner out of his pocket. With one hand Alex grabbed Hymeron by the throat and slammed his head against the wall; with the other he struggled to tear the device from Hymeron's hand.

Alex heard the other boy gasping, felt him quickly jabbing him, and kneeing him. Alex gasped at the pain. How did the little boy know how to fight like that? Alex shifted strategies using his secret training from Twarbie to knock the stunner free and block Hymeron's attacks. For a moment, they both broke free and looked down at the stunner lying on the ground between them.

"Where did you learn to fight like this?" Hymeron demanded.

The kid's voice sounded so much harsher, even ruthless, to Alex. "Are you really just a kid?"

"Sort of. As a human, I'd be almost as old as you, but I'm not going to be a wimpy Kimley. I'm going to—" Hymeron dove for the stunner.

Alex dropped on his back with a knee. Did he hear something crack? He didn't want to hurt the boy, but Alex refused to let him control the situation.

The Kimley let out a muffled gasp of pain, and Alex scooped up the stunner. Swiftly, he rolled off Hymeron, backed up bringing the weapon to bear on the boy. A scary sight met his eyes.

The boy had pulled another weapon from somewhere, and it looked much more deadly than the stunner. The expression on the boy's face sent a chill down Alex's back. "What are you doing? We've been friends."

Sounding more like the little boy he'd come to like, Hymeron choked out words of denial. "I can't afford to have friends. They're a weakness."

Alex remembered Amable's instructions. He pushed the button. Instantly Hymeron collapsed.

Alex backed up against a wall and slid to the floor. He was free. Yeah, about as free as a moth in a spider web. How was he forced into the *t'wasn't-be* thing? Alex tried not to think about Hheilea. He couldn't be rational if he thought of her. His thoughts lurched to Twarbie and the secret time he'd spent with her. He couldn't believe how he'd grown to care for her. The memory of her burned in his mind and the music playing in his head died away. It wasn't her choice to be terrible. She wanted to be different and he wanted to help her, but she'd slammed the door on that possibility. Alex ground his teeth at the memory of her warning. He heard her voice again and almost smelled her fragrance. "Don't try and find me or help me. Remember, if my people the other Winkles know you're my friend, they'll force me to torture you to death, and I can't stand that thought. I'll just be how I'm expected to be."

Bashing his fist against the floor, he muttered to himself. "Twarbie might think she had no choice, but I do and I don't give up." He jumped to his feet and left the room.

When Alex shut the door of the storage room behind him he paused for only a second before thinking of Gursha and hoped she could help him with his strange hair. After that, he'd have to take things one step at a time. He vowed that no matter what happened he would stay in control. Alex remembered what he'd told Peter. "This is a chance for us to help other people." One thing he knew, it wasn't going to be easy. He'd gotten so many problems, and he was just getting started. The words of his father came to Alex: 'We all need help with the little we have, to do what we can.'

Author's Note

I hope you've enjoyed the novella 'Alex Twice Abducted' as much as I enjoyed creating it for you. In a novella, it's impossible to show the richness of a novel; therefore, I have included an excerpt from the novel *Alex Inner Voice* for you to enjoy.

You'll meet four friends you've already read about but you'll encounter one that you've never met. Maleky is a bad guy, who's in Alex's head and speaks to him. You'll see them come head to head in a most interesting situation.

Excerpt

While Alex slept, a breeze blew through the open window. In the twilight a slight figure with shoulder length white hair climbed into Alex and Zeghes' bedroom. The person shook Alex and in a quiet voice said, "Wake up, Alex."

Alex groaned and rolled over.

Zeghes slowly undulating in the air on the other side of the room said, "Hello. Who are you?"

Then he answered himself. "You're one of the Kimley boys, except you're not a boy. Why does everyone call you a boy?"

Alex groggily said, "What's going on?

At the same time Hheilea let out a surprised and slightly indignant denial. "I am, too, a boy."

Zeghes twisted in the air and swung his head back and forth. "Your body's different from Alex's and he's a boy. Your body's very similar to A'idah's and she's a girl."

"How do you know that?" Hheilea said, stepping back from Zeghes.

Zeghes swung his head back and forth. "When I move my head I'm looking at you carefully."

Awakened by the conversation, Alex sat up in bed. "He uses sound to be able to see in the water and it works in the air."

"But... But... my clothes—," Hheilea began to protest and Zeghes cut her off. "I can see through clothing very easily."

"Ahhh!" Hheilea ducked down behind Alex's bed.

"What is it about clothing? I don't wear any," Zeghes said in annoyance, swatting his tail against the air.

Hheilea stayed squatted down, arms crossed over her chest. "I'm used to seeing some species without clothes, but I'm not used to having someone look right through my clothing. I'm sorry Zeghes. My reaction must seem silly to you."

Slowly she stood up. Even in the dim, early morning light Alex could see the blush. "Zeghes, this is Hheilea. She's Hymeron's older sister. Please keep calling her Hhy. Kimleys are always in danger in our galaxy from individuals who act like sharks. Girls Hheilea's age are in even more danger. That's why she's supposed to be in disguise as a younger boy. Can you help us keep her secret?"

"I'll protect you from the sharks," Zeghes said.

"Thanks, Zeghes," Hheilea said.

Alex looked at Hheilea. "What are you doing in here?"

"I needed to talk to you, but it's after five in the morning now. You'll have your alibi."

In a moment, Hheilea climbed back out the window and was gone, leaving Alex puzzled about her alibi stuff as he quickly fell back to sleep.

Later, Alex stumbled into the cafeteria looking for something to wake him up. A'idah sat at a small table by herself, her head in her hands. Zeghes swam past Alex and said to him, "You don't look like you got enough sleep with Hheilea waking you up early this morning."

Startled, his grogginess shed, Alex started to speak. Zeghes wasn't supposed to use her real name. Someone was going to hear.

A'idah looked up.

From behind Alex, Hheilea said, "Good morning."

Zeghes said, "Good morning, Hheilea."

Maleky yelled in Alex's head. Stop him! Don't let people know her name! He continued to yell comments and instructions as the conversation continued around Alex.

"Zeghes, you aren't supposed to—," Alex began to say.

A'idah interrupted Alex. "Hheilea? Aren't you Hhy, one of the Soaley boys?"

Alex hurried toward A'idah as he hissed. "Zeghes, come here." Reaching a puzzled A'idah, Alex continued talking. "A'idah, Hhy is Hheilea in disguise. All of the Kimleys are in danger, but girls who are about to become women are in extreme danger."

A'idah jumped to her feet, knocking over her table. In a flash she was at Hheilea, hugging her. She turned back to glare at Zeghes and Alex. "We have to protect her. Zeghes, you can't say her real name where anyone,"

Alex stepped back at the intensity in A'idah's voice as she continued. "and I mean anyone, but us or her family might hear."

Zeghes came close and touched Hheilea with his beak. "I thought it was okay to share secrets within the pod."

A tear ran down A'idah's face as she muttered to herself. "It isn't going to happen this time." In a commanding voice she continued, "We can't risk her secret with anyone else." A'idah loosened her arm's hold around Hheilea just enough to switch to holding her with both of her hands by the shoulders. She spoke directly to Hheilea. "Who's the danger to you? Why are you in danger?" She finished with an emphatic statement, not waiting for any answers. "I'm not going to let anyone hurt you."

TL Walker, Author

Tim lives in Olympia, Washington. A grandpa, he and his wife enjoy their children, and grandchildren. He loves making great food and gets even more enjoyment from watching family and friends eat the food.

He began creating stories at an early age. One night his seven-year-old sister woke screaming and he went to comfort her. On the spur of the moment, the twelve-year-old Tim created a fantastical story for her, calming her with attention grabbing details. Tim has an even earlier memory of creating a story sometime between six and seven-years-old.

Tim's fascinated by everything from flowers to Genghis Kahn and sand to Mount Everest. He finds people particularly interesting, always on the watch for interesting features and personality quirks. If you come to his website and visit, you might find yourself in a book. He's active in local writing groups and a beta reader for other writers. You can find him at: tlwalkerauthor.com or by email at: tlwwalker@tlwalkerauthor.com

CPSIA information can be obtained
at www.ICGtesting.com
Printed in the USA
JSHW022127030323
38386JS00006B/26